Shannon McCrimmon

THE HEARTS OF HAINES SERIES

Book 1 - *Kiss Me Hard Before You Go*

Book 2 - *Like All Things Beautiful*

Book 3 - *This is Where We Begin*

Published by Shannon McCrimmon
www.shannonmccrimmon.com
www.facebook.com/shannonmccrimmonauthor

Copyright © 2015 by Shannon McCrimmon

This is a work of fiction. Names, characters, places, and incidents are either products of the author's imagination or are used fictitiously. Any resemblance to actual events or locales or persons, living or dead, is entirely coincidental.

All rights reserved. No part of this publication may be reproduced, distributed or transmitted in any form or by any means, or stored in a database or retrieval system, without the prior written permission of the publisher.

Cover Design: Popcorn Initiative • www.popcorninitiative.com

For Victoria and Ashleigh,
you are like all things beautiful.

"The best and most beautiful things in the world cannot be seen or even touched – they must be felt with the heart." - Helen Keller

CHAPTER 1

It had only been two weeks, and the rumor mill had exploded. Evie Barnes was the main subject, and no one in the town of Haines could stop chattering. Under the hair dryer and at the manicure station in The Salon, she was the hot topic of conversation. In Lindy's Grocery, her name was whispered with a hushed disdain, followed by a pitying sigh with a slow shaking of the head. Outside Henson's Pharmacy, townspeople stopped to gossip about her. News spread all over the small town of Haines that Evie Barnes was shacking up with a carny boy, and to make matters worse, she'd allowed side show freaks to stay in her daddy's old house.

Evie wasn't oblivious to the chatter. She couldn't help but notice people stopping to stare, talk and gawk at her like she was a prized pig at the South Carolina State Fair. She knew. A girl as smart as Evie knew when her name was associated with derelicts and someone from a house of ill repute.

"Bless her heart, since her daddy died she's all but gone down hill. First Katie McDaniels, now her," Evie heard one woman say to another as she made her way to Henson's Pharmacy.

"Her daddy is rolling over in his grave right now," the other woman replied, followed by a "humph."

Evie was tempted to turn around and spit on them but thought better of it. A reaction meant she cared, and as far as she was concerned, she didn't. She was going to stand tall and walk with her head held high. She had business to attend to, and things had to go on as usual. After all, she had a farm to run and a few more mouths to feed.

She pushed the door open to Henson's and walked inside, searching for a few odds and ends. Old man Henson greeted her in his usual way— with warmth and familiarity.

"Hey, Evie," he said. A few long strands of white curled at the end of his mustache, and his eyes crinkled as he grinned wide at her.

"Hi, Mr. Henson," she said with a smile. She liked the old man. He was one of the few people in town who couldn't care less about her new living arrangements.

She clutched her scribbled list, double-checked it as she searched the store for the items she intended to buy and then made her way to the check-out counter. She slid the bottle of Asprin, bag of Sugar Babies, box of Twinkies, and eight pack of glass bottled Cokes in his direction.

"You doin' good, Evie?" He pushed his glasses up on the bridge of his nose as he clicked on the keys of the cash register.

"Yes, sir." Despite the fact that she ached for her daddy, she was doing just fine. She had a new family who had helped fill the void in her life and a boyfriend who filled the hole in her heart.

"That'll be $4.98."

Evie handed him a crisp five dollar bill. She peered over her shoulder, in time to see Miss Sue scowl at her.

"Hi, Miss Sue," Evie said with a resounding sigh. She never cared for Miss Sue. Most people in town weren't too keen on Miss Sue either. She was a busy body with nothing better to do than stick her nose in everyone else's business. Most people clammed up when she came near them for fear that whatever they said would spread faster than wild fire.

She smacked her gums—several of her teeth were missing and those that remained were tarnished and crooked and plain nasty—

and frowned at Evie. "You oughta be ashamed," she hissed.

Evie was tempted to respond with a snappy comeback but decided against it. If Miss Sue didn't approve of her, then she'd take it as a compliment. What'd she care about the old woman's opinion anyway? She kept a straight face – one that didn't show the annoyance she felt deep in her core. As she headed toward the front door, she gripped the brown paper bag in one hand, and her free hand was balled into a tight fist.

"See you later, Mr. Henson," she said and glanced at Miss Sue, who was still glowering at her.

"Grayson Barnes raised you better than to be some hussy who takes in riffraff off the street," the old woman spat.

That was the final straw. Evie spun on her heels and faced her. "He raised me just fine, Miss Sue. Well enough to know when to keep my opinion to myself when something doesn't concern me," she said with a raised voice, feeling the blessed moment of triumph.

She shoved the door open and marched to her truck. Old cantankerous Miss Sue was most likely standing inside of Henson's with her mouth wide open, astonished that Evie had the nerve to talk back to her.

Served her right, she thought. Assuming about her daddy. If he was alive, he'd welcome them all into his home: Finch, Doris, Mouse, and Friedrich. Evie knew that for sure. Her daddy had a big heart, bigger than the state of Texas, and she sure as hell knew her father better than anyone in Haines, especially old crotchety Miss Sue.

She plopped herself down inside of her truck, started it up and drove toward home, muttering curse words as she poked along Main Street. That sweet moment of victory faded, and Evie brought her fingernails to her mouth and began biting on them. They had grown a smidgen since Finch had come into her life earlier that summer. He chastised her for chewing on them. "It's like eating rat poop," he'd say. "Your hands touch everything, Evie." But at that very moment all Evie thought about was her daddy, wondering just a little if maybe the townspeople were right.

***

Evie hurried up the front porch steps and opened the screen door. Music was playing on the record player – one of Gray's records. Katie was loudly humming along to the country western tune as she dusted the furniture. Rag in hand, Katie moved back and forth, polishing the antiquated table. Since she had moved in with Evie, she had taken on the role of housecleaner, telling Evie it was the least she could do since Evie had saved her from her dreadful father.

She took a good look at her best friend: her belly had gotten bigger. Katie was five months pregnant, and her clothes had started to pop. It was only a matter of time until Evie would find herself on a shopping trip with Katie scouring for maternity clothes that didn't look like burlap feed sacks.

Evie turned the volume down on the record player. "The dogs are circling," she teased.

"Ha, ha," Katie retorted. "I don't sing *that* bad."

"I heard pregnant women are tone deaf, but you take the cake."

"I've heard you sing, and your voice isn't much better."

"Where's Finch?"

"Outside." Katie turned the volume back up and sang louder than before.

Evie headed toward her kitchen, placed the bag on the table and made her way outside. Since Finch had moved in, he was intent on repairing everything that needed to be fixed. This included things that were fine as they were, but according to Finch, needed some improvement.

"It'll take you years, Finch, and by the time you fix everything, it'll all need it again," Evie had said.

"I'm not letting this place go to shambles," he had told her, and Evie realized that Finch was as stubborn about things as she was.

The scent of cow manure permeated as she trekked through the grass and headed toward one of the barns. This barn had been neglected by Gray years ago and wasn't used much except to store extra feed, tools and such. Evie said it was a waste of time, but Finch told her they could use it to hold the goats he was so intent on getting.

"What are we going to do with goats?" Evie caught herself using "we" a lot when she talked about things on the farm. "We" meant all of them, not just Finch and her, because the operative word equated the family she had just inherited.

"Goats produce milk, which makes cheese," he said, like it was the most obvious thing in the world.

"Duh, I know that," Evie had responded. "But no one drinks goat's milk," she scrunched her face, "and goat cheese is gross. Besides, Daddy used to sell cow's milk, and it costs too much to keep a dairy farm, Finch." She had hoped that he'd listen. When it came to agriculture, she knew what she was talking about, and even though Finch had ideas, some of them needed to stay as ideas.

She continued walking and saw the speck of him off in the distance. The sun reflected off of his warm olive complexion, and as she got closer, she stopped to stare.

His shirt was off, and he held a paint brush in his hand, going up and down in one fluid stroke. Evie saw his muscles moving. *Lawd have mercy.* He's like a dish of butter. She laughed at her ridiculous thought and then smiled at herself for sounding like her daddy. That's what he said all the time: "Lawd have mercy." Since he died, she picked up things he said or did, and she knew within a matter of years, she'd sound and act just like him. She was just fine with that. Just fine.

She snuck up behind him and wrapped her hands around his waist. His firm, flat stomach was damp with sweat, and he smelled like hay and the outdoors. She took a whiff, enjoying his scent. He was manly. If someone asked Evie to describe Finch's scent, she'd say just that.

He spun to face her, and let out a soft smile. "I knew you were coming, you know?"

"Yeah, right."

He tugged on her braid. "You could never be a spy."

"Maybe I am, and this is my cover?" She pulled away from him and glanced at the barn. "You writing while you're painting?" Half of the letter U and all of the letter T were painted in white.

"Yeah." She heard the lilt in his voice. He moved in front of the gigantic letters.

She peered around him, staring at the letters, then brought her gaze back to Finch and read his sorrowful expression. She brought her hand to her mouth and shook her head. "Lawd have mercy," she whispered.

He placed his hand on her shoulders and squeezed. "I didn't see it until you left for town," he said in an apologetic tone. "I was hoping to have this painted over before you got home."

"No sense in hiding it, Finch. Let the whole world know that I'm a slut." She threw her hands up in the air. "That's what was written, wasn't it?"

He paused and then finally spoke in a quiet tone, "Yeah." His eyes were downcast, and he pressed his lips together. "I knew I shouldn't have moved in with you. Whoever wrote it is going to pay." He tightened his jaw and clenched his fist.

"No sense in going all Michael Corleone."

She peeked at the barn again and let out a laugh. Finch gave her a confused look.

"It's kinda funny if you think about it."

"How is any of this funny, Evie?"

"Me, a slut? Last time I checked you have to sleep around to earn that title."

"I told you living with you was a bad idea," he said. "The town thinks I'm shacking up with you." He kicked the ground and grunted. He liked living there, holding her at night and being with her, but he didn't like the repercussions.

"Well, you are shacking up with me." She smiled and then grew serious once she saw he wasn't going to change his mind. "You think some stupid head writing the word 'slut' on my barn is going to upset me? You don't know me that well, then," she said with her head held high. "Paint over it, and let's forget it happened."

"Evie, it's only going to get worse."

"Well, we'll just have to deal with it, won't we?" She titled her head up, looking at the painted barn. "Why white anyway?"

"It was all I could find." He shrugged. "And I wanted to paint over it fast."

"You can't protect me from the world, Finch."

"But I can at least try, can't I?" he said with an earnestness that made Evie want to kiss him.

"You always said you wanted a red barn," she said, raising her brow. "How about starting with this one?"

He smiled at her in admiration and cupped her chin. "You've gone and grown up, Evie Barnes."

"Need some help painting?"

"No. I'm good." He tugged on her braid one more time.

She pursed her lips and furrowed her brows. "Why do you do that?"

"I don't know." He rolled his shoulders. Sure, he knew why. She was just so darn cute he couldn't help but touch her when he was around her, even if that meant pinching her nose or tugging on that cute braid of hers.

"It's like being back in elementary school."

"I would have been in the principal's office all the time if we had been in school together."

Her eyebrows squished together. "Why's that?"

"Because I wouldn't have been able to stop poking you, pulling on your braid, just doing something to get you to notice me," he said with a lopsided grin.

She placed her palm on his sweaty coarse cheek. "I definitely would've noticed you."

He tugged on her shirt and brought her to him. He wrapped his arms around her, placed both of his palms on her cheeks and leaned forward, pressing his lips against hers and kissed her gently. He pulled away and smiled. "You taste like Sugar Babies."

Her eyes peered down, "I may have had one."

"May?" He laughed. "I just tasted nothing but caramel."

"Fine." She waved her hands up in the air. "You win!"

He laughed again and pulled her to him. "Oh Evie, you make me smile."

"Because I like Sugar Babies?" she teased.

"Yep, and that's the only reason."

CHAPTER 2

He finished painting the last strip of wood on one side of the barn and placed his paint brush on top of the empty can of paint. He wiped his forehead with his forearm and pulled his t-shirt over his head, putting it back on. This wasn't going to be the end of this nonsense: painting barns to cover up hate, because that's what it was – pure hate.

He wondered if he had made a mistake in coming there, settling on her land as if he belonged. *Did he belong anywhere*? He had spent all of his twenty-two years of life wandering from place to place never really staying put long enough to call anywhere home, and now all he wanted was to do just that, but at what cost? If it meant Evie would be ostracized by the community, he wasn't so sure he was willing to take the risk for her sake. It was all about her now. Every decision he made was about her.

"You're in deep thought tonight," Friedrich said, approaching him. He took one look at the barn and then pinched his brows together. "White is not a good color for a barn."

"It was the only paint she had, and it needed to be done quickly." He breathed and added, "I'm going to paint it red anyhow."

"Red is a more suitable color for a barn," Friedrich said. He chewed on a piece of hay and flashed a toothy smile.

Finch found the corners of his mouth curling up. Friedrich had taken to the farming life – giving into the stereotype that farmers wore overalls and straw hats and chewed on hay.

"I like that look, Freddy. You could start a new sideshow: Tattooed Farmers."

"My showing days are over," he said with a proud smile.

Out of Doris, Mouse, and him, he had become the most content never to stand before a crowd again. It surprised them all. At one time, Friedrich was the most vocal of them all, cherishing the moments when he stood before crowds who were enthralled by the spectrum of colors that covered his muscular body. He loved to flex his muscles, show off his tattoos and lift heavy items above his head. And he was the real deal, too. While some carnivals allowed hacks to pull the wool over the eyes of crowds by lifting styrofoam filled items created to look like heavy objects most men could not lift, Friedrich picked up steel, iron and other heavy elements not meant for a man's hands.

He was the one who stood outside, calling in the crowds so he could wow them into silence. He was the one who talked Doris into joining the circuit, telling her that her lovely curves were the perfect addition to his show. They'd met one night after he'd dropped a heavy barbell on his foot, which shattered his bones into pieces. He was sent to the hospital and cared for by Doris, who was the night shift nurse. Her girlish twang soothed his pain, and her smile was what lured him in. It didn't take long, maybe an hour or two, but within that time, he was smitten.

It didn't take much persuasion. She was searching for something different and wanted to get out of that no good for nothing town of hers in the middle of Texas. She hated the heat and was tired of seeing the same ole faces day after day. Faces that sneered at her and shot her dirty looks because she was larger than life – in all aspects. So she took him up on his offer. She quit her job, and her showing days began.

After only one week on the farm away from all of the hoopla

and crappy living accommodations, Friedrich's mind had changed. He didn't long for the attention, for the thrill of amazing others with his talents and skills. He wanted to live out his days on this farm, working with the docile cattle and living with the love of his life. To him, that was perfection.

"I love these cows. They are gentle in spirit and smarter than you would think. Doris just says I'm in love with them because I like big things," Friedrich said, raising his brows up and down.

Finch rolled his eyes. "Write it in your diary." He picked up the empty can and paint brush. That was his typical response to Friedrich when he started getting mushy about his relationship with Doris. He didn't need to hear about it if the picture was already painted in front of him.

He started toward the main barn with Friedrich in tow.

"When you buy that red paint, let me help you paint. Two of us will get it done faster," Friedrich said.

Finch moved close to him and lowered his voice, "I need you to keep an eye on things when I'm in Florida."

Friedrich gave him a skeptical yet concerned expression.

"The barn didn't need a paint job," Finch confessed. "I was painting over some stupid words."

"Words?" Friedrich repeated and then rubbed the indention in his chin.

Finch let out a breath. "Some idiots wrote some pretty detestable things."

"Like?"

"'Slut' and 'whore,'" he said with a deep breath. "With Evie's name in front of them."

Friedrich frowned. "That is terrible."

"And untrue. Stupid pricks don't even know what they're talking about." He shook his head in disgust.

"People assume what they want. That's why assume is spelled the way it is – makes an ass out of you and me."

Finch offered him a faint smile, but he wasn't in the mood to laugh or find humor. The situation was dire in his opinion, and anyone who'd go after Evie was the lowest form of human life in his opinion.

"It does not make it right, though, does it?" Friedrich placed his hand on Finch's shoulder.

"No, and I hope it doesn't get worse. She means everything to me. I can't ruin it for her."

"You are not ruining anything for her. This is those fools' problem, not yours, Finch."

Finch shook his head slightly and sighed. "I know. I hope this is the extent of this bullshit. Otherwise, it's going to be an uphill battle I'm not so sure I can win."

"You only lose if you give up, and I don't think you are a quitter."

***

They were circled around the dinner table eating dinner. It was a pleasant late summer's night, nice enough to open up all the windows and let the dipping temperatures cool off the room.

"It was hotter than a waiting room in Hell earlier today, and now it's cool enough I need a jacket," Mouse complained.

"Get used to it," Evie said with a groan. "The weather is moody."

"Like a woman on her cycle," Katie added.

Evie knuckled her in the arm. "Ick."

Katie winced. "Not the knuckles." She kicked her in the shin, and Evie grimaced.

Katie held her hand up and raised a brow. "You wouldn't kick a pregnant woman, would you?"

"She's going to use that as an excuse until she gives birth to it," Evie said to them all.

"It?" Katie said with protest.

"Fine. Him or her," Evie said.

"Him," Katie said with confidence. She patted her stomach and smiled. "He's definitely a boy."

Doris grabbed a roll and slathered butter on it. "So y'all are going to Gibsonton in a couple of days?" she asked and stuck the roll in her mouth.

Finch nodded.

Evie wrinkled her forehead. "I just hope the old truck makes it."

"It'll make it," Finch said, but even he doubted the truck's stamina. He'd just about put every bandage he could on it. "Quit being such a worrywart."

"Y'all sure you're okay managing the farm?" she asked Doris as her eyes wandered to Friedrich, Mouse, and Katie, checking for their reactions.

"Oh yeah, Honey Lamb. Ain't nothing to worry about," Doris said with a full mouth. Evie saw pieces of the roll inside of Doris' mouth as she continued to chew. "Those ole cows have become smitten with Friedrich, but that doesn't surprise me. He's a hunk." She waggled her thin painted-in brows. Evie thought it was strange that Doris kept wearing excessive makeup like she did when she had a show. She'd see her out there taking care of the cows wearing her pink frocks and her hair all teased just like she did when she was on the circuit.

"They're smitten with you, too," Friedrich said to Doris, and Mouse rolled his eyes.

"You think this is bad? Try living with them. That house is small even for me," he said.

Friedrich, Mouse and Doris had moved into the other house on the property that Katie had stayed in when Evie was sheltering her from Nate McDaniels. The confining two-bedroom house was barely big enough for Evie, Gray and her mother when she had lived there as a child. Evie knew that it definitely wasn't roomy enough for someone Doris' size. Add two more people and it was like squeezing the cows into the holding pins.

"Quit complaining, Mouse. It's better than that hell hole you slept in down in Florida," Doris said and narrowed her eyes to Evie. "Speaking of which, y'all are gonna pick up our things, right?"

"Yes," Evie answered.

"Good. Couldn't stand for my stuff to be there when someone else takes over the lease," Doris said. "I'm sure Kip will rent it out to some poor ole rube who doesn't know any better."

"Does he own half the property in town?" Evie asked.

"Just about, Honey Lamb," Doris answered. "Bought these dinky duplexes that ain't worth spit and rents them out to the likes of us who ain't got any other choice." She pursed her lips. "They're real shit holes too. But what else would you expect from the likes of him? He's all about saving a buck or two." She took a look around and smiled wide. "I sure like it here, though. Ain't ever felt like I could call a place home until I got here. It sure is nice picking out curtains and such." She laughed, and Evie smiled. "Got me some blue gingham fabric the other day and made it into drapes."

"I'm glad you feel at home," Evie said.

"I felt at home the moment we stepped on this land. Always did. Just kept going in circles until we finally found our way back here," she said. "So what are y'all going to do down there in Florida?"

"See the beach," Evie answered her with a wide grin. "Finch better take me, or he's in for a world of trouble." She narrowed her eyes to his and flashed a fake scowl, then smiled.

"Yes, yes." He patted her on the arm, and she swooped it away from him. He smirked and added, "It's all you've been talking about since I mentioned going down there." He was trying to feign annoyance. Truth be told, he liked seeing her get so excited over something, and that something happened to be the Gulf of Mexico, which was all Evie could talk about since he asked her to go with him to Florida. Plus, he didn't mind the idea of seeing her in her swimsuit. He wasn't a perv, but he wasn't dead either.

"There ain't much to the town, Honey Lamb," Doris said. "So, don't get your hopes up."

"She's right. There's nothing but a bunch of old retired carnies and circus people," Moused said. "Watch out for some of them, though; they aren't all nice, especially Nikko Andropolous." He shuddered.

"Who is Nikko Andropolous?" Evie asked.

"A crazy freak you shouldn't be alone with," Finch answered

"He's got one hell of a temper, and when he drinks, he's even worse," Doris said. "He'll go up and down the street with those claw-like hands of his, punching the air and shouting, 'Sonny bitch.'"

"Claw-like hands?" Evie said with a contorted face.

"Like a lobster almost. He's got two fingers the shape of a lobster claw," Doris explained. "He's The Lobster Man," she added without much enthusiasm.

"Really?" Evie leaned forward, placing her hand under her chin. Katie did the same and gestured for Doris to continue.

"Ain't much to say about him. He's a rotten son of a gun. He used to be on the circuit with us, but he got into too much trouble, fighting townies and all. Landed in jail in one town 'cause he got into a bar fight. Used to be a real big hit, but he was quite the hellion and ruined his career. Last I heard, he was working in Wes Wheaton's carnival." She twisted her lips to the side.

"Is that bad?" Evie asked.

"It's the same carnival Finch's daddy works in," Doris said.

"He's not my daddy," Finch clarified. "Yes, Evie, working in Wes Wheaton's carnival means you've hit rock bottom."

"Oh," Evie breathed. She never brought up Finch's father to him. All she knew was that they barely spoke and that Finch had gotten money from him to save the farm. For that, she was grateful even if the man had nothing to do with his son all of those years. At least he had the decency to give him money when he asked for it. Finch told her that was the last time he would ever see David Mills, and that was fine with him.

"I think Wes fired Nikko," Finch said and turned to face Evie. "Just stick close to me. I don't like that guy. Never did; never will."

Evie shivered and said, "You're giving me the heeby jeebies."

"Good. You need to have a little fear of some of those people," he said.

***

Later that night as they lay in Evie's bed, Evie grabbed a hold of Finch's hand and squeezed. "You're a walking contradiction, you know?"

He rolled on his side, facing her. "How's that?" He stroked her cheek with his finger, thinking she had the softest skin. It was like touching silk.

"You say you love me because I don't judge, yet tonight you told me to be afraid of 'those people.'" She emphasized the last two words.

Finch sat up and turned on the bedside table lamp. "Evie, you haven't seen the things I have or met the people I have, and I don't ever want you to."

She lay her head on his lap and ran her fingers through his brown shaggy hair, waiting for him to continue.

"Some of those people are not good for you to be around," he said.

She sat up and shook her head. "You did it again. Saying 'those people' like they're some sort of disease. You can't have it both ways. Telling me that you love me because I don't judge but making sure to point out that some of them are just plain bad. Which is it?" she raised her voice.

"Shh," he said. "You'll wake Katie."

"I don't care!"

"Why are you getting so upset?"

She folded her legs to her chest. "Because you're judging, like the way we're being judged. If the town took a few minutes to get to know all of y'all they wouldn't be saying the terrible things they're saying. Let me formulate my opinion and think what I want about whoever I meet because if I had listened to all the stupid heads, y'all wouldn't be living here and you sure as hell wouldn't be in my bed right now!"

He swallowed and let what she said sink in and stared at her intently, thinking he had fallen madly in love with the best person he'd ever met in his life, and he wasn't going to screw it up.

"You're right," he admitted.

"Can you say that again? I didn't hear you," she softened.

"No," he teased, pulling her to him and holding her as tight as he could.

"I love you, and I don't want to fight."

"You know what the best part about fighting is, don't you?" he asked, kissing the top of her blonde locks. He took a whiff, smelling the sweet scent of honeysuckle. He loved that shampoo of hers.

"No."

"Making up," he said and pressed his lips against hers.

CHAPTER 3

They were headed down to Florida, driving on I-26 and then onto I-95. Their windows were rolled down, and the radio blared old tunes that Gray had loved. Evie's bare feet rested against the dashboard. She wiggled her toes and let out a giggle. The oscillating fan moved around, circulating warm air.

"Your feet are getting the dash dirty," Finch teased, tugging on one of her braids.

She playfully punched him in the arm. "I'm going to stop wearing my hair in braids if you keep doing that!"

He raised a brow, knowing that she would in fact do just the opposite. Every time he did it, she'd giggle and playfully hit him. He knew that she loved him touching her hair as much as he loved touching it.

She inhaled, smelling the salty air. "The air smells different."

"Like a sauna with sulphur," he said with a crinkle in his nose.

"You don't like it down here, do you?"

He shrugged his shoulder. "It's all right I guess. Not like home." He formed a crooked smile, the kind that said "I'm all yours if you'll have me," or at least that was how Evie read it. And she'd definitely have him, no questions asked.

She melted from his words, thinking that she could indeed spend the rest of her life with this handsome guy sitting next to her, and she was fine with the predictability of their future together. Just fine.

"The grass is always greener," she said.

He turned his head and smiled at her, then focused back on the road. "I've seen enough grass in my lifetime. I know when it's green enough."

"You sound like an old man," she said. "Whoa is me, I've seen so much in my lifetime. I used to kill bears with my bare hands as I walked in ten feet of snow on my way to school," she kidded.

"And mountain lions, you know, because so many live in Florida," he shot back. "And we'd get so many snow days, too." He cocked a brow and tipped his head as if to say, "your move."

"It *could* snow in Florida," she muttered.

"Sure, up in the panhandle, maybe."

She grunted.

"You all right over there?" he asked.

"You get me so frustrated," she groaned.

"When you get mad, that little vein," he said, grazing her neck with the tip of his index finger, "pops out."

She swiped his finger away. "Sometimes I think you get me riled up for fun," she huffed.

He laughed loud. "You're so easy to upset. I can't help it."

She shook her head and tightened her lips, trying so hard to keep a scowl on her face, but when she turned her head slowly to the left, all she saw was Finch's brown eyes blinking bashfully at her, and the anger disappeared.

"You're going to see some strange types in Gibsonton," he said.

"Yeah. I figured."

"No, I mean, *strange*," he emphasized the last word and narrowed his eyes to hers for a brief second before bringing his attention back to the windshield.

"Stranger than you?" She smirked.

"Even stranger," he shot back.

"Good, because obviously I like strange people."

"Like or love?"

She shrugged and played with her fingernails. "Hmm... Maybe just like," she teased. He tickled her on the leg and under her arm. "Finch! Stop it!" she giggled.

"Admit it, or I'll keep doing it."

"Fine." Her face was three shades of scarlet. "I love strange people!" she hollered at the top of her lungs. "Are you happy?"

He smiled wide. "Yep."

***

The small town of Gibsonton was south of the city of Tampa and sat right off of the Hillsborough Bay. Warm year round, there wasn't much to the town other than the eclectic group of people who lived there. Established by two former side-show freaks, it was a refuge for current and retired carnival and circus employees. It was all Finch had ever known and the only place he called home when he wasn't traveling with the carnival.

Evie stared out her window, seeing trailer after trailer fill the flat, grassy land.

"So, what do you think?" Finch asked. A gentle tepid breeze blew through the truck. Evie watched palm trees sway with the wind.

She tried to think of something good to say, but such pleasantries escaped her.

"It's flat," she said. That was the truth. The land was different than Haines: no rolling hills or mountains in the distance. Just palm trees, sandy soil, and flat, flat land.

He laughed and patted her on her leg. "Such a bad liar."

She puckered her lips and thought long and hard for a moment, then shifted so she was facing him. "There's just not much to it."

"What'd you expect? Circus tents, flashy signs and rides everywhere?"

"Well, yeah, pretty much."

"It's our nesting place, Evie. It's where we live during the winter, and that's all."

"You keep saying 'we,'" she said.

He rubbed his hand across his lips. "Yeah. Guess I need to stop doing that, huh?"

"You can't forget where you came from, otherwise you'll never know where you're headed."

"Still. I'm an aspiring farmer now." He flickered a grin.

She peered out the window, seeing rusted carnival rides that were no longer good for use and old signs that took up most of the space on the lawns. A lion, tethered to a long, skinny pole, roared as they passed by.

"Is that what I think it is?" She stuck her head out the window and continued to stare at the spectacle as Finch drove on.

"Yeah. That's Neely McGrath's pet lion."

She plopped back down in her seat and scratched at her temple. "Pet lion?"

"He worked in the circus. The lion went with him when he retired," he said with a shrug. "Angus Patrick has an elephant."

"And this is the norm?"

"Oh yeah." He made a quick right turn down another road and pulled onto a short, patchy concrete driveway. "We're here." He gestured to a white concrete block house. Evie thought it was plain as could be. There weren't any shutters, and there was absolutely no landscaping. One laurel oak tree sat in the middle of the yard surrounded by overgrown weeds and a few wildflowers. The front porch was nearly bare with just two upholstered chairs. No potted plants. No wind chimes. Not even a welcome mat. Just nothing.

"That's my place." He pointed to a two-story garage that stood behind the home. It too was painted white and needed some tender loving care. They got out of the truck, and Evie placed her hands on her hips and took a good look around. A long row of white homes filled the gravel road.

An older man opened the front door. A ball cap hung lopsided on his small head. His trousers were pulled up to the middle of his stomach and were too short for his height. White socks were exposed, which were a stark contrast to his black-as-night tennis shoes. A cigarette dangled from the corner of his mouth, and his shirt was buttoned at the top and unbuttoned toward the midsection of his body.

"Finch," he said with a thick accent, which made him sound like he sneezed instead of saying Finch's name.

Finch smiled. "Rolf." He walked over to him, clasping onto Evie's hand as he did so. He shook Rolf's hand, gave him a quick side hug and pointed to Evie. "This is Evie," he said, beaming.

Rolf shook Evie's hand vigorously. He released his tight grip, and the blood began to rush back into her hand. She scanned him up and down. For his age he was in good shape, and she could tell that at one time he had been well-built.

"Finch has told me all about you," he said, and Evie cocked a brow at Finch.

Finch's cheeks turned ruddy. He peered down at the ground and kicked back and forth. "Yeah, well…" he began but was bumfuzzled for words.

Evie smirked, enjoying the sweet moment of Finch's

embarrassment.

"I made sun tea. Come in out of this dreadful heat and have some," Rolf offered. He held the door open as Evie and Finch stepped inside.

The house smelled of cigarette smoke. The floors were terrazzo, like those in a grocery store, and all of his furniture was upholstered in bold fabrics: gold, red, and purple. An oscillating fan hummed in the background, emitting just enough cool air to make the room bearable. Evie and Finch sat down on the gold sofa, facing a wall filled with framed pictures of Rolf's carnival days.

"My homage," Rolf said, noticing that Evie's blue eyes were glued to the cluttered wall. He handed them both a glass of tea.

"Thank you," Evie said. "Is Finch in any of those?" She squinted her eyes to get a better look.

"Of course." Rolf nodded and walked quickly to the wall. He took down three framed pictures and brought them all to her in one stack. "This is Finch when he threw knives," he said, pointing to the top picture.

Finch was dressed in a western style shirt and a pair of denim jeans. His dark brown hair was cut short and buzzed on both sides of his head, and baby fat lingered in his chubby cheeks. His expression was serious, and he stood in a wide stance with his hands on his hips.

"Look at you," Evie cooed. "You were so cute."

Finch rolled his eyes. "Rolf, you're killing me here." He tried grabbing the frame from her lap, but she brought it up to her chest and covered it with her folded arms.

Rolf laughed, then coughed again. "This one was right before Finch quit knife throwing," Rolf said with a frown. His eyes

LIKE ALL THINGS BEAUTIFUL **25**

appeared distant as if they were deep in reflective thought.

Evie turned to Finch. "That was before your mom."

Finch blinked, and his lips cast down.

Evie carefully placed the picture down on Rolf's coffee table and peered down at the last one in her lap. This one was of Finch and his mother.

Finch leaned over and gazed at the picture. "Mom," he said quietly and ran his thumb over the glass. He hadn't seen a picture of her in almost a year. He remembered her, often thinking of her on those long summer days, but seeing her image made her more alive somehow.

Evie handed it to him and said, "She was beautiful."

He looked up at Evie with a hint of dampness in his brown eyes. "Thanks."

"You look a lot like her," she said.

"He looks more like his father. Unfortunately," Rolf chimed in. He put out the nub of his cigarette and lit up a lit up another, blowing out a puff of smoke. "He only got his spirit from his mother."

"It is unfortunate, isn't it?" Finch said. "You try to forget someone, and every time you stare at yourself in the mirror all you see is their face staring right back at you."

"Life is irony," Rolf said. He sat down and crossed one of his boney legs over the other. He moved his head from side-to-side and brought his hand to his chin. "In your last letter to me, you said you were finally leaving the business," he said to Finch.

"Yep," Finch answered with a wide, confident grin. He placed the framed picture on Rolf's coffee table and brought his hands up to the back of his head. "Already left."

"I wondered how long it would take you," he said.

Finch gave him a questioning look.

"You had a knack for knife throwing but always seemed to want more," Rolf said.

"Because I did want more," Finch answered. He always knew there was more to life than just traveling from one place to the next. He wanted love. He wanted permanence. He wanted something to call his own.

"And you found it?" he asked.

"Yep." He wrapped his arm around Evie's shoulder, and she blushed from his overt affection. "I'm taking up farming, too."

Rolf let out a loud laugh and coughed. He leaned over, clutching onto his chest and cleared the back of his throat.

Evie turned to Finch with wide eyes.

Finch waved his hand down and shook his head. "He's fine," he quietly uttered.

"Now that is something I'd like to see. Is he good at farming?" Rolf continued, looking at Evie.

"Sure," she said with a lilt, and Rolf cocked an eyebrow. "He's learning," she added.

"Your mother would have found this very amusing," he said to Finch.

"I'm sure she would," Finch said.

"How long are you kids here?" Rolf asked.

"We're probably going to leave tomorrow," he said, and Evie let out a grunt. "But not before I take this one to the beach." He pulled Evie closer to him.

"Everyone should see the ocean, and one day is not enough time for a stay," Rolf said. "You can stay here as long as you like. I wouldn't mind the company."

"We'll see..." Finch's voice trailed off. Evie searched Finch's eyes for an answer, and he quickly darted his eyes away from hers.

Rolf finished his cigarette and got up. "Are you hungry?"

Evie nodded, and Finch said, "I could eat."

"We'll have to go out to eat. The maid quit. There's no food to eat here," his hazel eyes danced as he said it. "I'll drive us." He picked up his keys and jingled them, gesturing for Evie and Finch to get up.

"Rolf, maybe when we get back you'll show me your James Bond collection that Finch told me all about," Evie said.

Rolf stopped and thrust his chest out. "I will be proud to," he said as he rocked on his heels and spoke with his hands. "It is like nothing you've ever seen."

Evie stepped outside and pulled on Finch's t-shirt. "Why are we leaving so soon?" she whispered.

He half-shrugged. "There's nothing here, Evie."

"You grew up here. I'd say there's plenty. Quit being a stupid head," she said.

CHAPTER 4

As they pulled into the restaurant parking lot, Evie's eyes widened as an older naked man approached them. Every inch of his raisin-like skin sagged, and a large bald eagle tattoo filled his bare boney chest. Sprinkles of white hair covered the rest. He formed a shit-eating grin. A good bit of his teeth were missing.

He tapped Rolf's burgundy Buick passenger door. His long thin fingers drummed against the metal door, and he peered into the window. "That you, Finch Mills?" He squinted his beady eyes and leaned forward, moving his head from side-to-side. "Hi," he said to Evie.

Evie realized her mouth was still wide open, and she closed it, biting down hard on her lip to keep herself from laughing.

"Hi, Dick," Finch said with a sigh. "How are you holding up?" he asked, and Evie let out a low, quiet laugh that only Finch heard. He glanced over his shoulder and quickly shot her a look.

"Good. Just out for my nightly stroll. Nice night, isn't it?" He peered up at the cloudless sky and brought his gaze back to Finch. "Well, I gotta be gettin'. The wife made lasagna. Nice seeing you," he said as he moved away from the window and trekked back down the main road.

"Looks like a full moon tonight," Evie quipped and started to snicker.

"You're twelve, you know that, right?" Finch said, shaking his head and trying oh-so-hard not to laugh along with her but so help him it was funny. What Evie must have thought: seeing lions and naked men all in the course of one day.

"He was naked, and his name is Dick," she said, still giggling.

Her cheeks were red, and she couldn't stop chortling. He loved that bright-eyed, bushy tailed pure innocence about her.

"Dick likes to be nude," Rolf said. "I don't let him sit on my furniture when he comes over. I tell him to bring his own chair to sit on."

Evie laughed hard again.

Rolf had to park down the street away from the restaurant because the parking lot was full. Only one of three restaurants in town, Showtime was the first choice among locals because the food was half-way decent and alcohol of every variety was served. You could order a BLT and a pitcher of beer all for less than five dollars, and that suited the locals just fine. Tourists usually stumbled in, more interested in seeing a few side-show freaks than buying some grub, so the place didn't suffer for business.

A painted mural covered the outside of the restaurant: a collage of circus and carnival life. The collage was a tribute to those who lived there. Rolf boasted that he was in the mural and told Evie, "If you look closely, that's me, and that little boy right there is Finch." He pointed to a stick figure of a man who held a knife in his hand—aimed and ready to throw—and was standing next to a dark-haired little boy.

"Don't be impressed, Evie. He knew the artist who painted this," Finch said with an eye roll and opened the door for her. "Stick close to me, okay?" He pulled her close to him and wrapped his arms around her waist. So help him the last thing he wanted was for some drunk ass carny to say or do something inappropriate. He already felt like a jerk for bringing her to this dive.

"We're not in a war zone, Finch." She pushed his hands away and sauntered to an empty table. She sat and pointed to the empty chairs beside her.

He brought his free hand up to his nose and covered it, breathing through his mouth. The stench of alcohol, day old piss, and stale cigarette smoke permeated the stifling air, sickening his stomach. An Elvis Presley tune played on the jukebox, and a few drunk carnies swayed like marionettes on the open floor space, groping each other as patrons watched.

Finch scooted next to Evie and searched the bar for old friends and old enemies. He brought his arm around her and leaned close. He wanted people to know that they were together. That they were a couple, so hands off. Some of the lowlives that hung out there didn't have manners. They didn't have much couth.

"You looking for someone?" Evie asked.

"No," he said. What'd he care who was there? Enemy or friend. This was his past now. It was time for him to shut the door.

Rolf made his way to the bar and ordered a pitcher of beer. He tried juggling it and three glasses while he headed to the table. Finch got up and took them from him.

"I had it," Rolf said.

"Sure you did," Finch said. He saw that age had finally caught up to the once spry man. He shuffled when he moved and stumbled on his words. Finch heard the hesitation when he told stories, searching for words and names. And his hearing wasn't as sharp. It was all part of the life cycle, but it still didn't make it any easier for Finch to stomach. Rolf was his family.

"Finch didn't come in here much when he lived here," Rolf said to Evie. He lit a cigarette and took a long, hard puff of smoked filled air.

"Why not?" Evie asked, leaning forward.

"His mother cooked, and then she taught him how to cook," he said. "He hates cigarette smoke, too."

"I bet she was a good cook," Evie said. "He's pretty decent." She winked at Finch and smiled.

"She was," Rolf agreed eagerly. "Maggie could whip up anything and make it taste like it came from one of those fancy restaurants."

Finch stood up and stretched. "I'm getting us some Coca Cola," he said to Evie and headed toward the bar.

"He doesn't like talking about his mother," Rolf whispered. "He always changes the subject or walks away when anyone brings her up."

"Why?" Evie whispered back.

"Too painful for him I imagine," Rolf said with a frown. "They were tight, closer than most sons and mothers are, I suppose, but they were all they had. When she died, a part of him did, too. She was just a child when she showed up at Kip's carnival."

Evie gave him an inquisitive look, the kind that said, "Go on, please." She'd been dying to hear more about Finch's mother. Every now and again, Finch would share a tidbit or two, but not enough that she really felt like she knew the woman. A woman who had so much influence on his life.

"Real skittish thing, too. Like a mouse. Her parents kicked her out because they caught her with her boyfriend in the Biblical sense, if you get my meaning?" He arched a brow and waited to see if Evie caught on to his meaning.

She nodded, which gave him the signal.

He shook his head and peered down with a sad expression. "Why anyone would think it was justifiable to leave a seventeen-year-old girl helpless is beyond my understanding but people can be wretched creatures."

"Is that how she ended up in the carnival?" Evie asked.

"We were in her home town in North Carolina. She stayed after and begged Kip for a job," he said. "Got down her knees and folded her hands like she was praying to him. That fed his big ego, of course. I just felt sorry for her." He inhaled his cigarette and squinted his eyes. "Kip had a soft spot for her and decided she could stay on with us. He didn't need the help, but for some reason he always had a weakness when it came to her."

"Is that when she started knife throwing?" Evie placed her hands under her chin and tilted her head to the side.

He took a huge sip of his beer, like he hadn't drunk any liquid in a long time and swallowed hard. "No. She worked concession, but that wasn't enough for her adventurous heart. So, Kip moved her to repairs. She could fix anything, better than Finch, even. He's good, but Maggie was brilliant. There wasn't anything that she couldn't make better. But that wasn't enough for her either," he said. "That's when I took her under my wing."

"To knife throw?"

"Yes, and she caught on quick. She had a good aim and a lot of strength in those small arms of hers." He frowned again and sucked on his cigarette.

"But?" Evie asked, reading his thoughtful expression.

"That's when Finch's father came into the picture." His lips twisted to the side in disgust. "He was too old for her and knew exactly what he was doing. Like a predator almost."

Evie sat back against her chair and made an "o" face with her mouth.

"David was just as handsome as Finch. The difference was, he knew it and used it to his advantage. Finch has confidence, but David was arrogant. There's a difference," he said. "He had his eyes on Maggie and didn't stop pursuing her until he got in her pants."

Evie tried not to look shocked, but her red cheeks and wide blue eyes showed she was.

"Sorry," Rolf said. "I forget how to talk around women."

"It's okay."

"He left for another circuit once she got pregnant. Held Finch once or twice maybe when he was a baby but that was all." He scratched at his head and added, "I remember one time when Finch was a baby, he was crying real hard because he was hungry or tired, things that make babies cry," he explained, "and David just handed him over to me like I was supposed to make him stop. I told him to feed him, and he just shrugged and said he wasn't cut out for it."

"That's awful," Evie said. She now knew what it meant for Finch to ask his father for money to save her farm. She'd never in a million years be able to repay that kind of sacrifice. A warmth came over her as she realized the weight of Finch's love for her.

Rolf gently patted her on the hand and gave her a "there, there."

"He came around every now and again, but he never owned up to his responsibilities," he said. His thin lips cast down and his nose crinkled. "After that, it was one long string of bad men, worse than David." He leaned forward, glanced over his shoulder at Finch, who was at the bar speaking with someone, and whispered, "That scar on his arm. He got that from one of her lousy boyfriends."

Evie brought her hand up to her mouth. "How?"

"Archibald was a terrible man. The meanest snake of a man I've ever met." He shook his head slowly. "He was a mean drunk and had a penchant for hitting. Everything set him off, and when it did, he'd punch whatever or whoever it was: animals; women; children. One night..." he wiped a few tears from his eyes. "I won't give you all of the details, but when Finch found his mother knocked unconscious, he had enough. Archibald was just stronger than him."

Evie's hand lowered to her chest, feeling the beat of her hurting heart. She wanted to run up to the bar, wrap her arms around Finch and tell him it was going to be okay. That whatever horrible things life had thrown at him were gone and he was with her now. He was safe and sound.

"Archibald cut Finch up pretty bad. We had to take him and his mother to the hospital. You know Finch was only twelve-years-old at the time? Too young to fight battles like a man," Rolf said quietly. "It wasn't a good place for a boy with a big heart to grow up. He was cynical about life and people until he met you."

Evie dabbed her eyes with a napkin. "I can't take credit for that," she murmured.

"Yes," he firmly placed his hand on hers, "you can. You're his saving grace. I'm glad he's finally found a home. And someone to love."

Finch walked to the table carrying two glass bottles of Coca Cola. "Look who I found." He smiled and gestured with his head.

Stoney offered a grin to Evie, who sprang up from her chair and gave him an unexpected hug. "It's good to see you," she said.

He stepped back and gave a nervous laugh. "Didn't know I was the type to be missed."

He sat in an empty chair and lit up a cigarette.

Finch turned to Evie and whispered, "You okay?" He stroked her arm.

"Yes," she said, and they all started talking.

***

After sitting for hours in Rolf's house, listening to stories Evie enjoyed hearing, Evie and Finch made their way up the stairs to his garage apartment. The two-hundred square foot space was big enough for a twin bed, a shelf with an album collection that made Evie drool and a table with two chairs. It was clean, sparse and sterile.

"Good Lord, Finch, this place is depressing," she said, noticing there weren't any curtains hanging in front of the windows. There wasn't much on the walls: a few posters here and there, but not enough to make it look decorated. There weren't any plants in the window sills. Nothing to warm the place up and make it feel like a home.

He half-shrugged, lacking any comeback.

"You slept here?" She pointed to the narrow twin bed.

"Yep." He searched his shelf for an album and pulled out Simon and Garfunkel, placing it on his record player. Paul Simon and Art Garfunkel's voices filled the cramped space singing "El Condor Pasa." "This is my favorite," he said, almost dream like. He turned to Evie and added, "It makes me think of the good things from my childhood. Mom loved Simon and Garfunkel. She'd play this record over and over again, and I hated it. I'd cringe when she'd put this darn record on but now when I hear it, I smile. I can't help but smile."

"Dolly Parton is like that for me 'cause of Daddy. He loved her, and all I can think of is him when I hear her. It's a nice kind of hurt, you know?"

"That's the best kind," he said and sat down on his bed. He

patted the empty space in front of him, gesturing for her to join him. "It's the kind that makes you feel alive. I felt that when I left you," he confided.

She tilted her head and waited for him to continue.

He took a hold of her hand and laced his fingers in hers. "It killed me to be away from you, but when we'd talk and you'd read me the letters you never sent, it made the pain disappear."

"Those were the longest days of my life. I kept waiting for nine o'clock to come and when it finally did, it went by too fast. Time flies when you don't want it to," she said.

She sat cross-legged, scanned the room and crinkled her nose.

He reached over and pinched her nose. "What are you thinking about?"

"This." She motioned to the room. "It's just…" words escaped her. "Really depressing."

"Thanks."

"Sorry. I just expected more. Maybe some life to your home. Something that shows who you really are. The Finch I know."

He raked his fingers through his long shaggy hair. "Evie, I told you, I never had a home until I moved in with you. This was just a place to lay my head at night for less than half of the year. I know it's hard for you to grasp because you've never lived the Gypsy lifestyle, but that's basically what I was living for twenty-two years."

She thought about everything Rolf had told her, all of the horrible stories, the things he had to endure, and she couldn't help it. She reached out to touch him, grazing her fingers across the stubble on his face. She didn't say anything and moved her fingers across his cheeks, from his ears to his chin.

He placed his hands up to hers and kissed the tips of her fingers.

"What were you and Rolf talking about?"

She shrugged. "Nothing." She couldn't make eye contact. One look in his brown eyes, and she'd confess. She'd tell him everything he'd ever want to know.

He brought his hand to her chin.

"Evie," he said.

Her face turned red. "He told me about your mom."

"I figured as much," Finch said with a sigh. "And?"

Her brow wrinkled, and she bit on her lip.

He waited.

"He told me about Archibald," she said with a deep breath, like she had just spilled her guts.

Finch chewed on the insides of his cheeks and thought long and hard for a moment. "Archibald isn't even worth talking about," he hissed.

She couldn't stop the tears from falling. God help her, they were flowing like a waterfall, and the more she told herself to stop, the faster and harder they fell.

"Evie," he said in a thin voice. "Don't cry."

"I can't help it," she said, sniffling.

"Why are you so upset?"

She wiped at her damp face and stared into his eyes. "I just hate that horrible things happened to you."

He moved closer to her and hugged her tight. "Horrible things have happened to you, too, Evie. I got past them; so have you. Don't feel sorry for me," he said in a soft tone.

She pulled away from him. "I just love you is all, Finch, and it hurt to hear those things."

He offered her a faint smile and quietly said, "You make up for all of it."

***

She tugged on his Iggy Pop t-shirt and padded through his shag carpet barefoot. "It fits," she said.

He'd never be able to look at Iggy Pop the way same again. It was worse than the green night shirt that drove him wild. The dim overhead light shined down on her golden hair as she exited the bathroom.

Barely, he thought. "Yeah." His voiced cracked like a pre-pubescent boy.

"Thanks for letting me borrow it."

She inhaled, lifting it just enough that he caught a glimpse of her underwear. Were they floral? He swore he saw roses.

She smiled. "It smells like you."

"I didn't know I had my own scent." His voice was normal again.

She grinned wide. "Of course you do." She lay down beside him. Their two bodies squished together in the twin-sized bed.

Finch wrapped his arms around Evie and inhaled, smelling a fresh bouquet of flowers. To him Evie smelled like roses and other pretty things. He loved her scent, and there were those few times when she had borrowed a shirt of his, he'd sniff it over and over, hating that he'd have to wash it.

"I can't wait to see the beach," she whispered. "Daddy always wanted to take me, but we never had the time."

He kissed her on her hair, smelling that shampoo of hers, thinking that her wet locks felt great against his lips.

"He'd be glad I'm going," she said.

His mind drifted, and he thought about Gray and their last

conversation before he died.

Finch was milling about the carnival, checking the rides to make sure things were running smoothly. Gray had tapped him on the shoulder. "Got a second?" he had said.

Finch was no dummy. He wasn't going to say he was busy working. He'd make time for Evie's dad. And a man as tall and big as Gray wasn't a man anyone said "no" to anyhow.

"Yes," Finch said and swallowed. It'd only be a matter of seconds until he'd start sweating as much as Richard Nixon during his debate with John Kennedy.

"Things are getting pretty serious between you and Evie," he had said.

"Yes sir," Finch said, remembering that adding a "sir" with Gray was as important as remembering to wash his hands for a full thirty seconds after he used the restroom.

"I was right skeptical at first." His lip twisted to the side. "But you seem like you've got some sense, and I know you're treating her right."

Finch blinked. He wasn't going to argue, and he sure as hell wasn't going to agree. He knew that wasn't a statement he could agree to, otherwise it'd make him seem like a jerk.

Gray poked Finch in the chest, harder than he meant to because Finch flinched. The man had quite the jab on him.

Gray noticed his reaction and back peddled a step or two, just enough that there was a little bit of space between them but not so much that Finch felt comfortable again. He pointed his finger in the air; it was a smidgen too close to Finch's face for his liking. "I want you to promise me that you'll cherish her and treat her like she deserves to be treated. Evie's a hardheaded girl. And she's real smart, but she's real innocent about the world, too. I don't need her giving her heart to the wrong fella. You get my drift?" Gray had said, narrowing his eyes to Finch's.

"Yes sir," Finch said. "I care a lot about her." Hell, he might even love her, he had thought.

"Just promise me, you'll break things off if it ain't going to be serious. I don't want her to have a broken heart. It'd kill her." He frowned. "And she's too special of a girl to have that happen to her again."

"I give you my word," Finch said and brought his hand to his chest, his palm pressed hard against his heart. It was a lame gesture, but he wanted the man to know he meant what he said.

Gray nodded. "Good enough." He turned on his heels and walked off.

"You're quiet," Evie said, shifting so that their faces were within an inch of each other.

He stroked her arm and murmured, "Just thinking."

He pulled her closer to him, wanting to squeeze her and hold her tight. She was the only thing pure he'd ever had in his life, and he didn't want to mess up things between them. He was scared out of his wits that he was going to lose her because he knew if he did, he'd have too big of a hole in his heart that could never be mended. He promised her father he'd never break her heart. He wasn't going to muck this up—this thing between them.

"I love you, Evie," he said softly, so quiet she barely caught the words.

"I love you," she replied, just as soft.

***

The next morning as the sun was rising, they headed to the Gulf of Mexico. As soon as Finch parked the car, Evie dashed onto the sand, running clumsily toward the shore. She stopped to pick up some sea shells and dropped them in her pockets.

She tore off her shorts and t-shirt, showing a blue strapless one-piece that hugged tight against each curve of her body. Finch swallowed and skipped toward her.

"You gonna swim?" she asked. Her clothes lay in a pile on the white sand.

"I guess," he said. Swimming in the ocean wasn't his thing. He hated the stickiness of the sand and the salty water.

She tugged on his shirt. "Well, come on." She hopped in and splashed water up in the air. A look of amazement filled her as waves crashed against her legs.

Finch pulled off his t-shirt and stomped through the water, wearing an old pair of denim jeans that he had cut at the knees. He looked like an ass, he knew that, but why would he have a swimming suit. He noticed Evie's eyes stayed glue to his chest, and he thrust it out with confidence, glad that she, at least, thought he looked good.

The water was tepid, and the beach was free of anyone but them and a few older people shuffling down the shore holding metal detectors, searching for treasures. It was too early for sun soakers and kids to crowd the beach.

She swam further away from shore. The water hit her shoulders. Finch floated to her and stood on the sandy surface. The sand enveloped the creases of his toes, and the water hit him mid-chest.

"It is everything you hoped it'd be?" he asked. Even he could admit he was getting a little sentimental watching her blue eyes dance and that grin of hers spread as wide as it could go.

"Yes," she squealed and wrapped her arms around his neck, brushing the strands of wet hair away. "Wanna kiss?" she asked.

Did he ever? "You don't need to ask, Evie," he said and placed his hands on her small hips, picking her up so that they were eye-level.

She wrapped her legs around his waist and smiled all giddy, like a kid on Christmas day opening up presents.

His lips crushed against hers, and they kissed like no one was watching.

***

Evie sat slumped in Rolf's tattered chair, playing with the frayed piece of thread and winding it around her finger. She stretched her legs out in front of her and formed a dreamy expression. A warm breeze drifted through the front porch. Rolf sipped on his sun tea and then took a drag off of his cigarette. Finch was gone to Doris and Friedrich's old duplex, packing up the rest of their belongings.

Evie sat up and scooted to the edge of her chair as a colony of white, very long-legged birds waded past them. One of the svelte birds spread its wide wings. "Look at the size of that bird's wings." She turned to Rolf with an amazed expression.

"Great egrets. Pretty to look at," he said. "They come this way every now and again. There's a pond that way." He pointed. "They feed on the fish."

"I've never seen one in South Carolina."

"You probably won't up there in the mountains. Those are water birds." He got up, leaving his lit cigarette dangling on the edge of a small square table. Most of its white paint had been worn away revealing a thick coat of rust. "I'll be back in a minute."

Evie continued to watch the birds make their way through his yard and onto the next.

Rolf came back outside, carrying the three pictures he had shown Evie the day before. He handed them to her and said, "I want you to have these."

She titled her head, looking up at him with a soft expression. "They're yours. I can't take them." She tried handing them back, but he folded his arms against his chest. He pursed his thin, wrinkled lips.

"They're for you to have now," he said. "I'm too old to stand here arguing with a young woman. If I say I want you to have them, I mean it."

"But they're..." she started, but he interrupted her.

He placed his palm on her shoulder and looked directly into her eyes. "Finch is like a grandson to me. His mother was like the daughter I never had. An old carny like me doesn't get married and have kids. No woman wants a life with a wanderer," he said with a frown. "Life was supposed to turn out this way for me, but Finch, he's got a different journey. He was born to be a husband and a father. He deserves that much, and you're the first and only person that has ever come into his life that he sees a future with."

"Shouldn't you give these to him?" Evie asked.

He let out a sigh. "I know you're a smart girl. He wouldn't date a bimbo," Rolf said. "I'm giving these to you because you're so special to him, which means you're special to me too. You make him happy, and for that I'm thankful. I consider you family now." He took his hand off of her shoulder, and Evie latched onto it and squeezed. A few tears welled in her blue eyes. She was at a loss for words.

"Thank you," she quietly uttered.

"Now you have family pictures to hang up in that home of yours. Finch can't stop talking about it. He says it's the most beautiful place he's ever seen."

"It's not much," she said.

He patted her on the hand before letting go. "Never downplay what you've inherited. From what Finch has said, that father of yours was a good man, and you seem to know a thing or two about taking care of that gorgeous land you've got." He sat back down and finished off his cigarette. Evie held on tight to the pictures and brought them close to her heart.

"I'm glad he'll have a piece of his past."

"His life wasn't all good, but there were times, like those," he pointed to the pictures, "that were happy for him. Take care of him, Evie."

"I will. I promise," she said, hoping that the townspeople's prejudice toward him and the other carnies would disappear.

CHAPTER 5

Finch drove slowly. There was no hurry to get back. Evie had her cows to worry about, but even she could admit that taking a vacation away from them was good for the heart and soul. She thought about the times her daddy left with Cooper for his "man time." Now she got it. Everyone needed that kind of time, that kind of solace.

They were almost back home. She saw her house in the distance. On top of a rolling hill, it was hard to miss, standing grand and tall and surrounded by all of that land.

"They seem okay," he said, gesturing to the hungry cows that grazed on the grass and rested under shaded trees trying to steer clear of the summer sun.

Good, she thought. If things had gone well while she was gone, that meant she could take more trips like this. Not that she was rolling in the dough and could traipse around the country, but knowing that she and Finch could hop in the truck and go somewhere was enough of a thrill.

"Think anyone came to skate?" she asked as they passed the square-shaped slab of concrete. The rink hadn't had much business since the carnival accident.

"Probably not," Finch said with a frown.

Evie tried to let it roll off her shoulders, but losing the income from the skating rink was going to hurt down the road. She hated the town for their ignorance.

Finch pulled up the drive and turned off the ignition. Evie jumped out and placed her hands on her hips, taking a good look. Everything looked the same, but what'd she expect anyway? It's not like they were gone for weeks. It had only been three days. Just enough time that she finally got to see the ocean.

"Looks like Cooper's here," Evie said, gesturing to Cooper's beat-up pick-up truck.

Katie greeted them at the front door. "Y'all have fun?" she asked, wiping her hands on her red checkered apron. Dough stuck to her plump cheeks.

"Yes," Evie said.

"Good," Katie said with a grin.

"Your cheeks are all rosy," Evie said and wiped the dough off of Katie's cheeks.

Katie brought her hands up to her face and patted them, getting off any remnants of the sticky flour composition. "Must be the cooking."

"Hey there, Evie," Cooper said with a grunt as he heaved himself up from Evie's couch.

She smiled at him and then her smile grew wider. "Well, hey there, Preston," she said. "Isn't this a nice surprise."

"You're all grown up," he said and picked her up off of the ground, giving her a nice, tight hug. Any woman with any lick of sense would welcome a hug from Preston Dobbins.

He set her down safely to the floor and extended his hand to Finch. "Preston Dobbins."

Finch grabbed his hand and shook it. "Finch Mills."

"This here is my baby brother," Cooper explained to Finch.

Preston barely resembled Cooper. There was an age gap between them – large enough that Cooper could be Preston's father, and their hair differed in color. While Cooper's was more gray, Preston's was a nice light brown, the color of coffee and heavy cream. Their eyes were different shades. Cooper's were a basic brown; Preston's were just like his mother's: green. Greener than the grass outside. Greener than Ireland. They were the first thing someone noticed.

Beyond that there were even more differences. He towered over his older brother, and was half as round. And unlike Cooper, Preston had some fashion sense and wore a fitted button-up shirt tucked into a pair of denim jeans. On most occasions he wore a stetson hat, but since he was inside of Evie's home, it was off of his head and resting on the side table.

"Whatcha doing here, Preston?" Evie asked. She was trying to remember the last time she had seen him. A few years? He traveled around the state because of his job. Last time she saw him was at his parents annual barbeque where they shared one dance. The dance meant much more to Evie than it did to Preston. For weeks she thought about nothing else, wondering if they'd date once she grew up, but now that she was grown up, Preston and that dance didn't cross her mind.

"Just here to see the family. Had some vacation I needed to take or I'd lose it," he answered.

"Y'all staying for dinner?" Evie asked.

Preston turned to Cooper, who nodded vigorously.

"Guess that's a yes," Evie said with a laugh.

"Katie can cook," Cooper whispered loudly to Preston.

Evie noticed Katie turn crimson and gave her best friend a look.

They made themselves comfortable in the living room while Katie finished cooking.

"How was Florida?" Cooper asked.

"Great!" Evie said. "I got to see the ocean."

"About time," Cooper said. "Your daddy would be glad you

finally did. I know he always wanted to take you."

Evie decided to change the subject. Sometimes she could handle talking about her daddy; sometimes she couldn't. And today was one of those days that it pained her to bring him up. "So, Preston, how's life as a DEA agent?"

She was always intrigued by his job as a Drug Enforcement Agent. She pictured him on stake outs, arresting drug dealers and hauling people in who had broken the law. He'd served as a police officer in a neighboring county a few years before joining the agency.

"Good. Staying busy," he said.

"Turning in lots of crooks?" Evie asked.

He laughed. "Yeah, Evie." He smiled at her and his lips cast down. "I was real sorry I couldn't come for your daddy's funeral. I was in the middle of a big bust and couldn't get here. You got my flowers, right?"

She had gotten them. One dozen pink roses. That was Preston for you. Send her pretty flowers, not the funeral parlor type, at least that was what she called the bouquets filled with baby's breath, carnations, and other standard flowers. "Yes, thank you."

"And how are you enjoying farming life?" he asked Finch. "Coop told me you used to work in the carnival that came to town every year."

"Yeah," Finch said. "I'm enjoying it."

"He wants to get some goats and start growing tomatoes and other vegetables for profit," Evie said. That was the last discussion they had anyway. Finch was all about using the land, making money off of something other than cattle. The cattle weren't guarantees, he had told her. Well, neither were crops, Evie had said.

"That's a good idea. Y'all could sell to your local grocery stores," Preston said. "Raising cattle is a hard business. Just look at Coop," he pointed to him, "he's beekeeping now."

Evie and Finch both raised their brows.

Cooper gave his brother a stern look. "Didn't want to share that information until I got my first batch of honey."

"You giving up on your cattle? This is news," Evie said, scooting off of her chair and leaning forward.

"No. No." He waved his hand down. "I'm still raising my cattle. Just dabbling in some other things to occupy my time."

Evie stood up, and all of the men in the room got up. "Y'all can sit," she said. Old-fashioned manners hadn't died with the Dobbins men, and Finch, well, he surprised her sometimes. For someone who had lived a vagabond lifestyle, he sure knew how to be a gentleman.

"I gotta set some extra places around the table." Her face pinched. "Gonna be hard." She was already fighting for space with the six of them. Adding two more seats was going to be a tight fit.

"Why don't we eat outside? It's a nice enough night," Finch offered.

***

Finch had built the picnic table the first week he was there. Evie had no idea he was so crafty. The guy could fix and build anything, and there was proof of that around her home. Most of them sat at the picnic table, with the exception of Doris, Friedrich and Cooper, who sat nearby in lawn chairs.

"When are you due?" Preston asked Katie.

"About four months," she answered.

He tilted his head to the side and said, "You're having a boy."

Evie noticed that Katie's cheeks flushed.

"How can you tell, Preston?" Evie asked.

"The way she's carrying," he said. Evie knew if anyone was a seer when it came to pregnancy, it was someone from the Dobbins family. There were eight of them: six kids and Mr. and Mrs. Dobbins. Preston was the second to last born in the big family.

"She keeps calling him a 'he'," Evie said.

"It's good to talk to him. He can hear you." Preston flickered her a grin and winked.

"See." Katie gave an exaggerated look to Evie and then looked back at Preston. "That's what I've been telling her."

Evie threw her hands up in the air. "I give up!"

Katie and Preston laughed.

As Evie and the rest started clearing their plates, Evie pulled Katie off to the side. "Your face sure is turning red a lot tonight," she whispered.

"It's hot," Katie said.

"Hot if you're an Eskimo maybe. You were playing with that mop of hair earlier, and I noticed you thrust those big boobs of yours out," Evie continued.

Katie shot her a dirty look. "These," she glimpsed down, "can't help but stick out. When you're pregnant, Eves, everything gets bigger."

"Whatever you say. I know you well enough, and I can tell when you're flirting," she said, tapping her foot against the grassy lawn, waiting for Katie to confess.

"Eves, I'm pregnant, unmarried, and basically homeless. If I'm giggling more or got a red face, cut me some slack. I've been holed up here for months. I'm hot all of the time, so fat that I can't see my feet anymore, and my ankles are the size of tree trunks. So if some hunk of a man winks at me and I blush, so what." Katie stormed off.

Finch tapped Evie on the shoulder and whispered, "What was that all about?" He watched as Katie trudged into the house.

"I'm just a big dodo bird is all," Evie said. "Just a dodo bird," her voice trailed off.

***

Finch strutted down Main Street with his hands in his pockets and the sun beaming down on him. A few townies shot him dirty looks. He did his best to ignore them. He was used to getting the stink-eye treatment from pissed-off townies. He wondered how long this was going to go on. Nate McDaniels hadn't helped matters. That sorry sack of crap incited the town after the accident – an accident that Nate had caused, nonetheless. But that was brushed under the rug by the pansy sheriff, Winton Ford, who seemed to share in Nate's lack of ethics. Evie and Finch left Ford's office in frustration realizing that people like Nate rarely got what was coming to them.

Several rubes in the town were just ignorant enough to follow Nate and his ideals. He told them what they already believed anyway: carnies were loathsome sorts that brought havoc to good old-fashioned towns like Haines. The seedy stuff was already there, creeping around, but it was easier for the town to believe that Haines was full of good people and that people like Finch were bringing it down. He worried that this was going to continue. And how would that impact Evie?

Finch kept to himself, keeping his eyes straight ahead. He wasn't going to peer down and feel ashamed. He didn't have anything to be ashamed about. Let them make their remarks under the breaths and stare at him like he was the devil himself. He could take it.

He passed by The Diner while he walked down Main Street. One of the few restaurants in town, it was always busy. He side-glanced at the crowds who were enjoying a hot breakfast and starting their mornings off with a cup of coffee. A few people lingered outside, warming up the wooden benches and taking their time to start their day. Things moved slower in Haines. Slower than Finch was used to.

Nate McDaniels and Sheriff Ford walked out the front door of The Diner. Finch balled his hands into fists and picked up his pace. So help him, he didn't want to get near either one of them. But people can sense when you're trying to avoid them. And like animals, McDaniels and Ford slithered their way to Finch.

"You better not be causin' any problems," Ford shouted.

Finch kept walking, pretending the rube wasn't talking to him.

He heard Ford stepping up his pace and felt his hot breath closing in on him, creeping up against the back of his neck.

He poked Finch in the back, not too hard, but definitely hard enough for Finch to feel a sting.

"I'm talking to you, boy," he said. Finch hated the way he addressed him as "boy" like the prison cops from Cool Hand Luke.

Finch turned slowly and waited. His fingernails dug into his hands inside of his pants pockets.

"You better not be causin' any problems," he repeated. "You hear me?"

Finch gave a quick nod.

"We don't need no trouble here," Ford added.

Nate appraised Finch with an evil glare and said, "He and his friends are bringing this town down."

It was always the hypocrites, Finch thought. The ones who put on a "holier than thou" appearance but were rotting inside because they were just the opposite.

"Now Nate, we can't be making our residents feel unwelcome," Ford said, all tongue in cheek, a big hint of sarcasm coming through his tone.

"You ain't from around here, so I'll school you on a couple of things," Nate said to Finch. "Keep your mouth shut; then there won't be any problems. You stay put on that farm of Evelyn's and don't come around here. No one wants to be reminded that your kind has made themselves at home in my town."

"Ain't no reason for you to come to town now is there?" Ford added. "Just keep to yourself and don't cause no problems."

Finch blinked and started walking once he got the drift that they were done with their little spiel. Idiots like them weren't ever going to go away, and he'd be better off keeping his trap shut and walking the other way. Nate McDaniels had too much power in that town. He wanted to turn around and punch him. Right in his mouth. He'd like to break that jaw of his and make it so he couldn't talk, but that'd land him in jail and in a town like this, he'd rot in a cell without any hope for parole. Even if half the town hated McDaniels, they wouldn't want some carny beating him to a pulp. Hypocrites. All of them. He let it roll off of his shoulders and continued on his way to Mike's Garage.

He shouted over the 1950s tunes that played on Mike's radio. Mike rolled out from under an avocado green 1974 Ford Pinto wagon. The color alone made Finch cringe.

"Hey, Finch," Mike said. He turned down the music and wiped

his greasy hands against his grimy work clothes and smiled. "What can I do you for?"

"I have a business proposition for you," Finch said.

"Go on. I'm listening."

Ten minutes later, they shook hands, and it was decided that Finch would work at Mike's shop three days a week. Mike could use the help, and Finch could use the pocket money. First paycheck he received, he was going to take Evie out on a real date. He'd take her to see Grease, even though the idea of sitting through a musical was pure torture, but he'd do it for her. He'd do anything for her.

He whistled down Main Street. He couldn't help it. A man needed something to call his own. He was already driving her truck, living in her house and working off her land. He hated to think that way. Evie told him he was stupid whenever he did.

"You partially own it now, Finch. After all, you paid to save it. Hell, Doris, Friedrich, and Mouse have a say so now, too," she would say. But in his dark hard head of hair he still saw things his own distorted way. Plus, he was going stir crazy. Working the farm kept him plenty busy and fixing things around the farm occupied the rest of his time, but he wanted to do something he loved and that would put change in his pocket.

"There goes one of those carny freaks now!"

Finch turned. Most people in his shoes would. If someone is insulting you, you're more than likely to see who the culprit is. But twice in a day? This was getting old. Fast. And Finch's temper was sure to get the best of him in a matter of time.

He saw the kid, what was his name? Finch thought for a moment and tried to place the pimply-pizza faced kid. A lightbulb flashed, and Finch recognized him all at once, the chipped front tooth and bowl cut hairstyle. Logan Myers, the thirteen-year-old nuisance from next door. He was the little shit Evie loathed. He remembered her talking about how Logan and some of his friends rang their doorbell at four o'clock in the morning one night. She and her daddy knew it was him. Gray saw the scrawny kid running off with his friends, making noises like a pack of hyenas. When Gray called the Myers, they denied that their son could even do such a thing and said it had to be someone else. But Gray and Evie knew it was him.

He and his group of friends laughed, proud of themselves for their little insult. The friends were cheering on the brat for having the kahunas to stick it to Finch. "Way to go, Logan," one of them said. They were licking their ice cream cones, sitting on their bicycles, looking like a bunch of snot-nosed kids with vanilla ice cream dripping down their jutted chins. Finch wanted to take their cones and smear the ice cream against their acne-filled faces, but that'd only give them the juice that they needed.

"Go back to where you came from!" Logan shouted at Finch.

The hatred in his blue eyes even surprised Finch. How a kid could vehemently hate a stranger who had done nothing to him other than being attached to a carnival? But this wasn't the first time in his life he had somebody tell him to go back to where he came from. If only they knew: he wasn't really from anywhere, so he couldn't go back. To anywhere. Besides, he was home now, and he was staying put. No matter what.

He chose not to offer a comeback. No sense in getting into an argument with a bunch of teenaged kids who didn't have anything better to do than harass the likes of him. Better to take the high road and keep on walking. His temper had gotten him in plenty of trouble in his life.

He heard the little shit cheering with his friends, shouting "yeahs" and "way to gos!" Like they had just won the damn Superbowl. Proud of their triumph because they had conquered the carny.

Let him have his sweet moment of victory, Finch thought. He wasn't worth the trouble.

He drove back home, wiping out the incidents with Nate and the sheriff and the stupid kid and his friends. There'd be more of those, and he couldn't let it ruin his day. He had a part-time job now, where he could earn his own cash and spend it all on Evie if he wanted. He wanted to spend money on her and just spoil her rotten.

He parked the truck, seeing her petite frame far off in the distance in her denim overalls and her hair in braids. She looked so darn cute. Wearing those green work boots of hers and her daddy's John Deere ball cap. He loved that hat on her.

She jerked on her garden hose and sprayed a restless heifer. The stubborn heifer jostled, trying to break loose from the braided rope slung around its wide neck—the rope was double-knotted around a tree trunk to keep it from dashing off.

He was tempted to surprise Evie, but with a six-hundred pound heifer ticked off and close to her, there was no fooling around. "Evie," he called.

She quickly glanced over her shoulder and kept on spraying. A look of anger filled her, and she muttered under her breath. Finch knew her moods all too well. When she was mad, she puckered her lips and kept her head to the side. As Finch moved closer, he saw why she was so pissed off.

"I keep spraying her, and it won't come off," she said with a groan. The heifer was drenched and mooed, bucking forward. "Steady now," Evie said, but the heifer wouldn't listen. She patted it on the head and turned the hose off.

Spray painted red in big bold letters, the word "Trash" covered most of the heifer's wide body.

Finch untied the rope from around the tree as Evie gently took the rope off. The heifer ran past them, missing Evie by a few inches.

"You okay?" he asked. He asked because she was upset. He asked because that damn heifer almost knocked her down. He asked because it was becoming too much for her. He saw the strain in her face.

"Just mad as hell is all." She went to the spigot and twisted the knob to the side, turning the water off. "I don't know who is doing this..." her voice trailed off as she stared off at the painted heifer who was now grazing in the grass. "It's one thing to paint on my barn. It's another to paint on one of my heifers."

"Think it's Nate McDaniels?"

She stared up at Finch and twisted her lips. "The thought has crossed my mind," she said. "He wouldn't do this, but his stupid head cronies would. He's still trying to get my land."

Finch balled his hands into fists and cursed under his breath. Nate McDaniels was the bane of his existence. The man was pure living evil, and it seemed like nothing bad was ever going to happen to him for the sins he committed.

She pulled a golf ball out of her pocket and held it up. "And look at this. Someone's hitting golf balls onto our property. I found a few of these in the grass." She shook her head in frustration and let out a grunt. "One of the heifers acted skittish today. I think a golf ball may have hit her. I put some salve on her, but I don't know if it will help." She bit down on her lip.

"Maybe we should keep watch."

"Then what? Shoot 'em when we catch them?"

Finch cocked a brow. "It's not a bad idea," he said with a smile.

"Then we'll all be in jail, and then what?" She shook her head and kicked the ground with her rubber boots. "Dammit! They want us to get upset, you know? That's what this is all about. They want us to get scared, to run and give up. Well, I'm not a quitter!" She hollered to the sky.

He patted her on the shoulder. "We'll figure out who this is and put a stop to it."

"If it's McDaniels, there's nothing we can do." She frowned and let out a heavy sigh. "That man runs this town."

"Try not to worry. We'll figure this out," he said, but even he didn't know how they'd figure this out. Once they caught whoever it was doing this, what would they do? Threaten them? If it was McDaniels and his rotten crew, an idle threat wasn't going to ward them off. It'd take a lot more than that to get him to stop his hate campaign. Finch was going to put a stop to it somehow. One way or another, he couldn't allow this to continue happening. But he knew he was powerless. In that town, he was a nobody, an outsider, and any accusation against McDaniels wouldn't be believed or taken seriously.

"What have you been up to?" she asked. She was done discussing the matter, but her mind was still reeling. He knew because she chewed on her fingernail, and the way her blue eyes moved back and forth in thought. She was such a worrier.

"I got a job," he said, feeling pretty darn proud of himself. A real job. A job not associated with a carnival.

"A job?"

"I'm working a few days a week with Mike down at the shop."

She smiled. "Mike's plenty busy, so I'm sure he could use the help."

"Yeah." He nodded. "I'll still help out here."

"Just don't start bringing up goats again," she teased and then bit on her lip. "You didn't have to get a job, you know? What's mine is yours."

He pulled her to him and kissed her. Lightly at first, soft as a feather tickling her skin, but the longer their lips pressed against each other's, the stronger the kiss became. He wrapped his hands around her, holding her like he was afraid to let go. He nibbled her on her ear—kissing that freckle he loved so much. He loved holding her. Touching her. Being near her.

"Get a room!" Katie hollered from the porch as she shook dust off of a throw rug.

Evie pulled away, flushed. She tightened her lips. "Finch Mills, you have to quit kissing me like that!"

He laughed. He'd kiss her like that and then some.

"I want to work to make my own money, Evie," he said. "And whatever I earn is yours." She could have it all. He'd give her the shirt off of his back and one of his organs if she needed it. Whatever she wanted, he would give her. No questions asked.

He glanced at the painted heifer, thinking he'd keep watch every night until he caught whoever it was causing her so much pain. No matter what. He was going to put a stop to it.

CHAPTER 6

The Dobbins family barbeque was an annual event attended by most of the town of Haines. Fred Dobbins and his wife, Patsy, had an open door policy, so even loathsome sorts like Nate McDaniels attended. He was invited because of his wife Julia. Most people felt a tinge of sympathy for the poor woman: married to a selfish philandering man. Sympathy for her got them a lot of invites that otherwise would have been lost in the mail.

"I'm going to see my dad there," Katie sighed as she swept the kitchen floor.

"I know." Evie frowned. She knew it'd be hard on Katie. Anytime she bumped into him in town, Evie felt the aftermath for days. Katie's moods were swinging back and forth like a pendulum, and the further she got into her second trimester, the more she went from being happy one moment to a blubbering mess the next. Evie had recently made the mistake of taking her to see the movie *Superman*, thinking it was going to cheer her up to see the hunky Christopher Reeve in a tight fit costume, but Katie blubbered throughout most of the film. "I feel bad for Superman. He lost both his parents and his planet," she had said. Evie swore she wouldn't take her to anymore movies until after the baby was born.

"I could eat off of that floor, you know?" Evie said, watching her best friend sweep the same spot over and over again.

Katie held the broom still and looked at Evie.

"You cleaned it yesterday and the day before that," Evie explained. "This house is cleaner than it's ever been."

"So," Katie said. "That's not a bad thing." Her face was red, and her feet were bare. Katie had resorted to wearing flip flops— the cheap kind that anyone could buy at Henson's: plastic and worth about five cents, made out in some dingy factory somewhere in a third world country. She had gone through four or five pairs now, and the more pregnant she got, the bigger her feet did, too.

"You can take it easy," Evie said. She was starting to feel bad about it all, about Katie cleaning so much when she was over five months pregnant.

"Take it easy. I'm not dying, Eves," Katie said with a laugh. "Just pregnant." She moved the broom back and forth against the linoleum floor. "And this gives me something to do."

All Katie wanted to do lately was housework, and sooner or later, she'd find out there wasn't anything left to clean. Then what, Evie thought? Clean the inside of the barns? That'd be a sight. Her prissy best friend knee deep in cow poop.

Katie yawned and sat down at the breakfast table. "I sure would like to not look like a hippo at this barbeque." She gazed down at her bulging belly.

"You're beautiful," Evie said. It wasn't a stretch of a compliment. Katie was attractive with her dark silky hair and cute cherub face. Most people in town thought the same, too, and when they were in high school, most guys didn't mind taking a second look at her or flirting with her when Todd wasn't around.

Katie rolled her eyes. "You have to say that, best friends pact and all."

"You know if I thought you were ugly as sin I'd tell you."

Katie laughed and then yawned again. "That's true. You don't mince words."

"What about that blue dress?" Evie offered and found herself yawning, too.

"It's getting tight. Buttons are these girls own worst enemy." Katie glanced down at her ample chest.

"We'll find something," Evie said. "Why are you so intent on dressing up, anyhow?" Evie teased, raising a brow. She knew why.

Katie wouldn't make eye contact and mumbled, "No reason."

"It couldn't be because of a certain Dobbins, could it?" Evie nearly sang.

"No," Katie lied.

"You're lying." Evie pointed at her and smiled.

"Okay, fine, that's part of it," Katie huffed. "But Eves, there's going to be people there that we went to school with, and it sure would be nice to look them square in the eye knowing that I looked good and not like a sloppy, puffed-up blow fish."

"Well, we're just going to have to make sure you look gorgeous."

***

Doris straddled a chair, breathing hard and heavy, her belly rose, touching Katie's stomach as she applied make-up to Katie's face. The three of them were in Evie's bathroom. Evie was squished between them and watched as Doris did her magic.

"Honey Lamb, there ain't going to be a fella that doesn't do a turn around for you. I better keep a tighter rein on Friedrich. You better keep one on Finch, too, Evie," Doris said and giggled. "It sure is fun dolling you up. Blot those lips." She applied bright red lipstick to Katie's lips.

Katie heaved herself up off of the toilet seat lid and got a look at Doris' work, checking her reflection in the mirror. She patted her cheeks and shook her hair, noticing the slight curls in her grown out Dorothy Hamil cut.

"You got nice legs, Honey Lamb," Doris said, pointing to Katie's tanned legs. "That dress looks good on you."

It had taken them hours to find that blue empire-waist dress with the cute little bow that tied in the front. Evie had all but given up, thinking there wasn't a stitch of fabric Katie would like, but Katie found the dress hidden on the sale rack, and Evie purchased it before Katie could change her mind.

"You look beautiful," Evie added.

Katie smoothed the dress down against her and smiled. "Thank you."

"This was fun," Doris said. "Let's all get dolled up for this barbeque."

Evie shrugged. Why not, she thought. They could all go there looking like a million bucks, and they may just need that confidence if there were any naysayers there.

***

Finch whistled, and Friedrich twitched his brows. Evie, Katie, and Doris came sauntering down the stairs, heads held high, and chests thrust out. Friedrich bent over and kissed Doris on the hand. "You look lovely, my dear," he said.

She waved her hand in the air. "You're making me blush," she teased, but Evie could see hints of rose on Doris' plump cheeks.

"You all look pretty," Mouse said.

"Thank you." Doris patted her shoulder confidently. "Y'all are with the best looking dames in town." She said with a confident nod. Her hair was teased, and she wore a pink bow in her curly brown hair. Katie had applied her make-up, so it wasn't as severe as she normally wore it. Her pink satin frock hung loosely against her skin. Since she moved onto Evie's farm, she'd shed a few pounds, enough that her clothes didn't stick against her rolls of fat anymore.

Evie ran her fingers through her feathered hair and grinned at Finch. His eyes scanned her from head to toe as she purposely swayed with a little more oomph than usual. She knew he was checking her out. She'd have to be blind if she didn't.

"Nice shirt," he said, grazing his finger across her arm. A trail of goosebumps formed up and down from her legs to her shoulders, and she smiled in self-satisfaction.

She was wearing a sleeveless button-up top that tied at her waist, showing hints of her tanned stomach. Her denim cutoff shorts hit her at the top of her thighs, and she tried to eloquently walk in her platform shoes. Anytime she wore shorts with platforms, Finch went crazy. Like he was right then: nearly salivating and eyes wide.

He intertwined his fingers through her belt loops and gave her a lopsided, boyish grin, the kind that Evie loved. "Nice shoes, too," he whispered.

"Ahem," Doris cleared her throat, and Evie and Finch turned to look at her. Everyone was staring at them, rolling their eyes and muttering under their breaths.

"Y'all are syrupy sick," Doris said and smacked her lips, like she had just tasted sour milk.

Mouse and Friedrich nodded in agreement.

"Try living here with them," Katie groaned as they headed out the door.

Squeezing six people into a pick-up truck was a feat. It was decided that Doris and Katie would sit up front with Evie, but no one gave any thought to the fact that there may not be enough room for the three of them.

The door handle poked into Evie's leg, causing an instant throbbing pain. She grimaced from the impact, as her legs pressed harder into each other when Doris sat down in the cab. With Katie between them, straddling the stick shift, Evie was glad that the Dobbins' farm was only a few miles up the road.

"You good?" Katie's arms were folded into her chest like a vampire sleeping in his coffin.

"Yeah," Evie said with an uneven breath. Only ten more minutes of constricted breathing, she thought.

***

Fred and Patsy Dobbins' old farm house was noticeable from a far distance. With its mustard yellow coat of paint and blue shutters, anyone within driving distance couldn't help but see it. Not that it was ugly, because it wasn't. Most farm houses in the area were white, but Mrs. Dobbins read interior decorating magazines and had painted the exterior more than a few times since she'd move in. It was always the talk of the town. What was she going to paint it this time? Locals would poke around, waiting to see what color she had in store for the old house.

The Dobbins' house was big, large enough to house six children. The land itself wasn't anything worth coveting. It didn't offer the same views Evie's did. It wasn't set on top of a rolling hill with a three-hundred sixty degree view of the mountains. It was possible to catch a glimpse of the mountains from one side of the property. The land was filled with cattle, and a powerful stench of manure often filled the farm on warm days. Still, it was pleasant enough.

The party had already started. A local band, most of which were volunteer firemen and some of the old guys from the VFW, played their guitars and drums, while Ernie, the lead singer, tried his best to imitate Elvis Presley. His voice was a tad too deep to replicate The King, and his leg looked more like it was having a spasm when he shook it.

Groups huddled near the band, clapping their hands and watching in awe. Entertainment was entertainment in the small town of Haines, and any form of it was welcome. Children played a game of baseball further away from the crowds, and the rest sat on lawn chairs, sipping on Patsy Dobbins' homemade punch, rumored to have enough liquor to light your pants on fire.

Evie held onto Finch's hand as they made their way to the action. He carried the ambrosia salad Katie had made, another hobby she had taken up. Evie swore she was going to get fat with all of Katie's cooking and then would gripe when Katie slid her plate of barely eaten food away. "I crave it and then it tastes bad," she'd say to Evie. They had several dishes of Katie's cravings stacked in the refrigerator.

"Coop, you cleaned up," Evie said, noticing that his hair was still wet from showering, and his clothes were pressed.

"Can't come over here looking like a slob," he said, motioning toward his mother.

Evie smiled, and Finch set the ambrosia salad down on the filled table, stacked with casseroles and other strange salads.

Doris beamed, waving at people who would just purse their lips and turn the other way. She shrugged her shoulders and said "Oh well," to Friedrich. A hint of sadness filled her voice. Since they had moved in, she'd tried to make friends with locals, but most hadn't given her the time of day. And a person as social as Doris wasn't cut out for isolation. Friedrich grabbed her by the hand, and they made their way to some empty chairs.

Mouse pulled on his suspenders and blinked his eyes. "Drinks are over there," Cooper said, noticing Mouse's small head moving side-to-side. Mouse gave him a quick nod and headed in that direction.

Katie played with her dress, and Evie nudged her. "What are you doing?" she asked.

"Nothing," Katie said and lay her hands to her side.

"Y'all sure do look pretty," Preston said as he approached them. He winked at Katie and flashed a grin, showing all of his perfect teeth.

"Thank you," Katie said with a flustered smile.

"Let's get a drink and sit down," Evie said to Finch and Cooper, wanting to leave her best friend alone with the man who seemed to have a hankering for women dressed in blue, or at least he didn't seem to mind Katie's company.

They found a few empty chairs next to Doris and Friedrich and took their spot under a big shade tree. Doris fanned herself with one of her old Japanese fans as Friedrich hummed quietly to the music. Ernie sang a slower tune, and a few couples swayed back and forth, moving to the beat of the song.

"I sure hope Katie's daddy doesn't come," Doris said. "She looks so pretty and seems to enjoy talking to Preston. Looks like some jealous girls are shooting daggers at her right now." She pointed to a few women who stood off to the side, glaring at an oblivious Katie.

"Nate is like those dogs that go around pissing on everything to mark his territory," Finch said, and everyone laughed.

Cooper spit chewing tobacco into an empty Coke bottle and said, "Preston ain't anything worth bragging about. He wet his bed until he was seven," Cooper said.

Evie playfully swatted at him. "You're just saying that because he's your baby brother."

Cooper didn't respond and spit into the Coke bottle again.

The sound of a bell ringing filled the night air, and everyone moved to the source of the noise. Patsy and Fred made a brief announcement, thanking everyone for coming. Fred said a quick blessing and motioned for everyone to fix their plates.

They waited in a long line, as hungry guests filled their plates like they weren't eating tomorrow. Or the next day. Or the next. Some pigged out more than others, stacking the food as high at it could possibly go.

"I didn't know she'd be here."

Evie tried not to glare at her, but sometimes it was hard to tolerate Jean Berry, one of the snottiest women in town, at least she was in Evie's opinion anyway, and most everyone else's, too. She had dated Gray back in high school, and Evie swore that the woman became bitter when he married her mother. Rumor was that Jean had planned their wedding after the first date and was heartbroken that Gray didn't reciprocate the strong feelings. Evie didn't like her tone of voice, or the way she was looking at them all, like they were cow manure on the soles of her shoes.

Jean shook her head slowly as she stared at Friedrich, Mouse, and Doris. Evie heard her "tsk-tsk" under her breath. "They just invited the entire town, didn't they?" she said with a huff to her friend, as if the Dobbins' had invited a pack of kids with head lice, spreading it amongst the guests.

So help Evie, she was going to grab a spoonful of potato salad and throw it at that woman's bouffant hair style. Stupid, stupid hair.

"If I had known this party was going to be so crowded, I would've declined my invitation," she continued.

"Then you would have been doing everyone here a favor." Evie filled the rest of her plate and stomped off in a huff.

Evie's ears were red, and her face was even redder if that was possible. She chewed on her food deliberately and complained under her breath. She ground her plastic fork into her thin paper plate.

"Doesn't know how to make friends, does she?" Finch teased and smiled.

"This isn't funny."

"Sure it is," Finch said. "Her car's in Mike's shop, and it looks like it's going to take longer to fix than I originally estimated." He gave her a wry grin.

"You're devious," Evie said. "Call me evil, but I like it." She giggled.

"I knew you associated with the dark side of the force," he kidded. "Should I worry when I go to sleep at night?"

"Yes. Sleep with one eye open, Finch Mills."

Their laughter was short-lived as Nate McDaniels' voice carried, and he became the center of attention for all of the guests at the party. Evie moved closer, standing behind a few onlookers. The music had stopped, and an eerie silence filled the festivities. Anyone within miles could catch bits and pieces of their conversation, and those who were in the front row were getting an ear full.

"You need to come home and quit living with those low lifes!" he shouted.

Katie fought back her tears, but Evie saw she was welling up fast. Now that she was pregnant, she sobbed at the drop of a hat. The other day she had cried because a dead squirrel lay in the yard.

Katie walked the other way, but he kept going at her, kept shouting at her, for the entire world to hear, or at least most of the town of Haines.

He yanked her by the arm, and his fingers dug into Katie's chin. "You need our help raising that baby," he said. "You can't do this on your own! You know you can't. You've never been able to do anything on your own."

Evie pushed her way through the crowd—she wanted to smack them all for standing there gawking at the train wreck—and rushed toward her best friend. Finch chased after her, afraid she was going to pummel McDaniels to the ground.

He secured his arms around Evie's waist and said in a low voice, "Don't, Evie. Don't do something you'll regret."

She jerked his hands away and snapped, "Let go of me." She caught up to Katie and took her by the hand, giving McDaniels the dirtiest, most foul look she could muster.

"You!" He jabbed his finger at Evie. "Are the problem. She'd be better off without you in her life, Evelyn," he spat.

"I think it's time for you to call it a night," Fred Dobbins said to Nate McDaniels. "Patsy is walking Julia out," he added and gestured for Nate to follow him.

"Katie, you cannot do this. You're not capable of raising a child. You don't have it in you," he added.

One last zinger, Evie thought. He had to get the last word. He had to say something that'd crush her spirit. He was the master at it.

Evie wrapped her arm around Katie's shoulder and walked with her far off on the Dobbins' property, away from the spectacle and drooling crowds who had watched the entire incident like it was good television. Evie knew just the place: the gazebo that faced the pond. She always liked that gazebo and had begged Gray to build one, but he'd always made the same excuse, "What are we going to do with that prissy thing?"

They sat down, and Katie rested her head against Evie's shoulder, sobbing uncontrollably.

"I." Sob. "Hate." Sob. "Him." Sob.

Evie combed her fingers through Katie's hair and tried to think of something consoling to say. What could she say? Sorry that your father is the spawn of Satan. Sorry that he is a good for nothing rotten S.O.B.

"I'm sorry, Katie," she said. It wasn't hurtful, and it was true. She was sorry, sorry that he was her father.

They sat there quietly. The band had started to play, and Ernie's voice carried as he sang a livelier tune, one that was was meant to bring life back to the party to forget the drama that everyone had witnessed. The clamoring and buzzing of voices filled the cool night air, and people began to dance, already forgetting what they had just seen.

Finch quietly approached them. He gave Evie a look, the kind that said, "Is she okay?"

Evie nodded reassuringly.

"Everyone's pigging out on that ambrosia salad of yours," Finch said to Katie.

"Good, 'cause right now I can't stand the smell of pineapple. I can smell it on you," she said with a pinched face.

He laughed. "And you thought my sense of smell was good?" he said to Evie.

"It's the hormones," Katie said.

"You want some dessert? There's cherry pie," he said to Katie.

"No, thanks. I think I'm going to sit here for a while," she said. "You can go on," she said to Evie.

"Are you sure?" Evie asked.

"Yes. Go on and fix yourself a plate of dessert," Katie said. "I'll be fine."

Evie stood up and grabbed Finch's hand. She looked one more time at her best friend, who motioned for her to get. She knew Katie wanted privacy. They started down the hill, and Preston met them half-way.

"Is she going to be all right?" he asked, glancing up at Katie, who was sitting in the gazebo staring off in the distance, with her legs swinging back and forth. She was so short her feet couldn't touch the ground.

"I think so," Evie said. She hoped so. She knew Katie was strong, but how much more could she take?

"You think it's okay for me to go over there?" Preston asked.

"Yeah, I think that'd be all right," she said.

He walked past them and headed toward the gazebo.

"I thought Katie wanted to be alone," Finch said.

Evie flicked him on the arm.

"Ouch," he winced.

"He's a man; she's a woman," Evie said in a tone that evoked, "Man, you're dumb as dirt."

"So," Finch said. "He's a lot older than her."

"He's not much older than her, and anyway, you're older than me," she scoffed.

"Not *that* much," he said.

"Shh." Evie stopped and placed her palm against his chest. "Did you hear that? He just made her laugh." She gave him a smug expression.

"Everything makes Katie laugh," Finch said and pinched her

nose.

"Did you really think I was going to punch McDaniels?" Evie asked as they strolled down the hill back toward the party.

"Yeah. I really did." Finch laughed. "Your hands were balled into tight little fists, and you had that look like you were aiming to kill."

"I wish I could punch him. I would if I could, you know? I'd punch him in his nose," Evie confessed.

"I know," Finch said. "Why the nose?"

"Because it would hurt," she answered, like she had thought about it more than once, which in fact, she had. "You think it's him that's causing us problems, don't you?"

"I'm pretty sure," he said. "He really hates you. He really hates us. It's like it's his mission."

"What is?"

"Getting your land," Finch said with a wrinkled brow.

CHAPTER 7

News of an "incident"—as it was referred by many—had spread across town. Everyone knew that Nate McDaniels had made an ass of himself at the Dobbins' party. What started as the truth turned into a wild tale with Nate getting hit by one of the carnies in a knock-down, drag-out type of fight without the boxing gloves.

Finch rolled his eyes at the gossip. As if Doris, Mouse, or Friedrich had it in them. They were as docile as anyone could be. Even Doris with her big mouth would run for cover the moment the shit hit the fan. Now him, he could believe they'd say that about. He'd been in a few fights in his lifetime; there was a year or two when it was the norm. He'd gladly hit Nate McDaniels. No second thoughts. He had wanted to hit him since he learned he was responsible for the carnival fire and the accident.

"Sounds like I missed a doozy," Mike said as they ate their lunch. This was their thing: take a lunch break at the same time every day and chit chat about nothing. Sometimes it was about cars, sometimes about farming; today was about the latest town gossip. Finch was surprised that he and Mike, who was about twenty years older, shared so much in common. An unexpected friendship had formed.

"Other than McDaniels putting on a one-act play, it was pretty tame. The food was good, though," Finch said.

"Dern shame I missed it then," Mike said and laughed. "You keep working as fast as you do and fixing these cars as fast as you are, people are going to expect the same of me, and what am I supposed to do on the days you ain't working here?"

"Well... maybe you should hire me full-time." He tried to sound like he was teasing, but an offer for a full-time job doing something he was born to do, something that came as natural as breathing, was just what he wanted. He could still help Evie out with the farm, and did he have plans, but this, this was what he wanted. He didn't know he wanted it until he had it. That was the way life worked sometimes.

"That ain't a bad idea. I'd say we could spit and shake on it, but we're eating."

"Since when did that stop you?" Finch narrowed his eyes to Mike's grime covered hands.

"True," Mike said with a laugh, and he spit on his palm— the liquid oozing down in a thick mass—and offered it to Finch. Finch mimicked him and shook his hand. And it was settled. Now he just had to break the news to Evie.

***

Doris stood outside the barn door, fanning herself. "Just can't handle it," she said with a crinkled nose.

Finch didn't ask and opened the barn door. A heifer lay on its side as Friedrich, Evie, and even Mouse worked to get its calf out. Evie's yellow rubber shoulder gloves were covered in a filthy slime, like she had dipped them in a bucket of mucous. She heaved, grabbing a hold onto the calf's legs, while Friedrich and Mouse held the heifer down. The veins in Evie's neck protruded, and her face was blood red. She pulled out and down, with one hand clasped securely around the calf's leg and the other around a doubled-knotted chain that was looped around the calf's fetlock and its other knee.

As the heifer took breaks, so did Evie. Finch felt like a helpless dope watching it all, but he had no idea what to do. Evie was working that heifer with skill and finesse, like she was doing a simple daily routine like brushing her own teeth.

"That's right. That a girl," she cooed, talking in a low, soothing tone, the kind you'd hear on late night radio. "Hold her steady," she ordered to Friedrich and Mouse. Finch squatted next to them and helped hold the tame heifer. "Pat her on the head," Evie said to them. "Talk to her like you want some loving."

"There, there, pretty little thing," Mouse said with his squeaky voice.

Finch eye-rolled him and said, "Good girl. You can do it. Just a little more." His voice was sultry and soft, a perfect blend to perk anyone up.

Friedrich patted the heifer's head and talked sweet to her. "That's right, Bertha, you can do this."

Evie grunted, pulled with all of her might, and the calf was born. She took the chains off of the calf. The cow bent over and licked its newborn calf. Its long, wide tongue covered the calf's body with sloppy kisses.

Their eyes were wide and dancing, amazed at what they had just witnessed. Friedrich clapped his hands together and sang jubilantly. "It's a miracle."

A few minutes passed as they watched the cow and her calf in amazement. Evie pulled the rubber gloves off of her and tossed them to the side.

Finch had seen plenty in his life, things that'd make anyone's stomach churn or belly laugh because they were so unbelievable, but witnessing the birth of a cow was remarkable. The fact that Evie did it all on her own was incredible.

Doris walked in, peering back and forth curiously.

"You missed it," Friedrich said.

"That's all right, Honey Lamb. I was just fine standing outside listening to all the hoopla."

Evie rinsed off of her arms and hands with the garden hose, scrubbing them with vigor. She shook them in the air, drying them off. "Well, that's that," she said. She brushed her hands against each other.

But Finch and the rest of them couldn't just blow it off like it was nothing. "That was amazing," Friedrich said. "I wish you could have seen it," he said to Doris.

Mouse nodded. "Papa never let me help birth our cows. He said I was too small."

"Well, it was something," Finch said and peered at Evie, who was watching them with her hands on her hips and her mouth twisted to the side.

"Why Bertha, Friedrich?" she asked.

He half-shrugged. "I have names for all of them. Her eyes remind me of an old friend."

Doris slapped him on the arm. "She better not be *that* kind of old friend."

"There's never been anyone but you," he said, and everyone in the barn groaned.

"Your old friend had big eyes," Evie said with a laugh. "And you know you can't name them all, right? They'll be going away. Bertha will be leaving in a week."

Friedrich and Mouse frowned.

She patted him on his arm. "It'll be all right," she said, but Finch saw a hint of sadness in those blue eyes of hers. "It's the way it is."

"Now I've got the blues," Doris said with a frown.

"We'll need to take turns keeping an eye on them." She pointed to the newborn calf and its mother.

"I'll go first," Friedrich said enthusiastically.

"Give it an hour or so and she'll be standing up."

"Amazing." He clapped his hands together and his eyes danced.

"You're pretty amazing with them," Finch said as he and Evie walked out of the barn.

"I'm okay I guess." She'd never really thought much about it. She didn't focus all her energy on how good she was at it. She just did it.

"Have you ever thought about becoming a veterinarian?" He'd thought of it for her. She loved the cows, and she loved her land, but he knew deep down she wanted more. She'd give hints, talking about ideas she had as a kid, things she wanted to do, to be, and he wondered why she never took the risk.

"A vet?" She laughed. "I'm not cut out to go to school that long, Finch. 'Sides, I'm not that good in science."

"What about a vet assistant? Like what Henry does for Tom."

She touched his stubbled cheeks and formed an appreciative smile. "That still requires some schooling, and I don't have the money to pay for it. And, I don't know how good I'd be with any other animal than cows. They're all I know."

"Don't people need help with their cows? Isn't there a job you could have where you could tell them what's wrong?"

There were jobs. She'd heard of agriculture inspectors who checked for bad beef. The work wasn't for the faint at heart. She'd have to dig into a dead cow's brains, but she could spot a sick cow a mile away. All of the people who had these jobs were old men, and last time she checked she was wet behind the ears and definitely not a male. Still, the idea of making some money for dispersing what she knew like the back of her hand was an intriguing one. She took a look at him and saw he was bursting at the seams to tell her something.

"So, you have something to tell me?"

"Yeah. I'm starting to think you've got a crystal ball."

She arched a brow. "And tarot cards, so watch out."

He laughed and told her about his new hours with Mike.

"I'll still help out here," he said. "And next spring, I want to grow tomatoes."

"You wanna fix things. That's what you're good at: fixing."

She took a deep breath and scrunched her face, pondering for a moment. "Finch, working on cars is perfect for you because there's something wrong with them and you can fix whatever it is." She inhaled and let out a loud exhale, like she was expelling air and her thoughts in one breath. "You got on this farm, aiming to fix everything; only thing is, some of it is just fine as it is. I've kept quiet because, well, a part of me felt like I should let you make some changes. But you can't douse a flower, Finch, or it'll die."

He got it.

"Y'all had ideals coming here, and it is what it is," she added. "I'm grateful, believe me I'm grateful, but too much change can be a bad thing. I lost Daddy and gained a new family in a year. Let's get these cows sold and then see. I can only handle so much."

He leaned over and placed his palm on her cheek. "I never meant to…"

"I know." She blinked. "I just want you to be happy, for us to work, because I love you more than anything in the world, but let's take baby steps, okay?"

"Okay."

"Good, now how about a swim in the pond?"

"A swim sounds good." He like the idea very much, so much in fact, that he picked her up off of the ground and spun round and round in circles.

"Finch!" she howled with laughter. "Come on!" she whined.

He set her down, panting like a dog on a summer's day.

"Last one there has to skinny dip." She grinned wickedly and zipped past a stunned Finch, who started after her, both of them praying to the heaven's above that the other would lose.

She won. Evie was a natural sprinter. Not athletic in the least, but after chasing cows for most of her life, she'd learned a thing or two about cadence.

He peered down at the ground and shook his head, muttering under his breath.

"Don't be such a sore loser." She laughed as she splashed water at him. She treaded in the water watching him like a hawk.

Man, did he wish he would have won.

He stripped down to nothing, bare as a baby just born. The wind crept up on him and he shivered a little. Fall was coming fast, and there wouldn't be anymore trips to the pond for a while. That made him sad. They'd taken to moonlight swimming, sometimes clothed, sometimes not. He cherished the times when they weren't.

He walked in backwards, glancing down at the weeds as he made his way in the water.

"I like this view of the moon better than Gibsonton's!" she said, giggling.

He swam toward her and splashed water at her.

"Finch!" she screeched as she wiped the droplets of water away from her eyes.

He tilted his head to the side. "Your shoulders are bare." He turned his head toward the shore seeing a pile of clothes off to the side. Her clothes. He gulped and looked back at her.

She gave him an impish grin and said, "I was hot from running."

Finch decided there and then that summer was his favorite season of the year, and he should encourage Evie to run more often.

***

They spent weeks sleeping with the newborn calves, nursing them, bottle-feeding them, treating them as babes in their arms. They took turns resting in the calf-hutch, talking sweet to the newborns to keep them calm. It wasn't much for sleeping, and the stench was overpowering, too much for a squeamish Doris, so much so that Friedrich took her shift. He relished in it all: a chance to live out on the land and experience all that life had to give them.

Evie had earned enough money, enough to scrape by for the year, but times were tough, and things were getting more expensive. She'd noticed that Henson's prices had gone up, and Finch said that even Mike was charging more at the shop. And soon she'd have another mouth to feed. Katie was due to deliver in three months. Maybe Finch was right. Maybe she should be a vet assistant instead of working like a mad woman day in and day out on her daddy's land. Since he'd mentioned it, the thought flickered in and out of her mind. She'd be cursing up a storm when a stubborn cow refused to budge, wondering if she was cut out for her daddy's work. Sure, she had what it took, but did she want it for herself the rest of her life?

She wrapped her sweater tight around her and patted Miles, her pet steer, on the head. He chewed on her tattered wool sleeves and lowered his head, waiting for another love pat. She obliged and sat on top of the fence rail, kicking her legs against it as Miles encroached her personal space and waited for more affection.

Finch walked her way, carrying a mug. She saw the steam rising from it.

He handed it to her and jumped up, sitting next to her. Miles nudged close to him, and Evie let out a humph.

"Traitor," she said to Miles.

Finch laughed and pet him.

She sipped and licked her lips. "Hot cocoa. My favorite."

"Katie made some," he said. "She's craving chocolate."

"Preston still in there?" She gestured to the house. He'd stopped in town for a night because he had just finished with a case in a nearby town and said he wanted to come over and say hi to them all. Evie knew that "saying hi" meant he wanted to see Katie.

"Yeah," Finch said.

"At least it's making her happy. That letter her daddy wrote her nearly sent her over the edge."

Nate had mailed a letter telling Katie she was no longer a part of the family, and he'd decided to disown her. He'd made a point to change his will and wanted nothing to do with her or that bastard child of hers. Evie couldn't believe the man had no soul, that he'd write his own child off like that.

What had upset Katie the most didn't have anything to do with the money. "He can have it!" she screamed to Evie. "But don't call my baby a bastard, like he's not good enough."

"I just hope Preston has the right intentions," Finch said.

Evie's brow wrinkled. "Why wouldn't he?" He was a good man. A standup guy.

He shrugged his shoulders. "I don't know. Most guys don't chase pregnant women."

"He's a good guy," Evie defended. All of the Dobbins men were. Preston wouldn't waste Katie's time. And as far as she knew there wasn't anything going on between them. According to Katie, they were just friends. But it seemed to Evie that he'd make excuses to come over there. One time with Cooper. Another time because he said his mom wanted him to bring over a peach pie. And then today because he said he had a recipe for her swollen feet. It was some salve an old mountain woman had given him that he swore would do the trick.

"I'm not saying anything bad about him, I just think…," he started, fumbling for words. "Maybe there's more to it."

"I think you're jealous because you know I used to be sweet on him." Evie laughed, noticing Finch's expression was still serious. She quit laughing and asked, "Are you? That was a long time ago."

"Am I jealous that you liked somebody when you were twelve? Evie, I'm jealous of any guy that you've ever set your eyes on. Even John Travolta, when you drooled over him in *Grease*."

"Well, he is hunky," she said. "And I caught you doing the same over Olivia Newton-John when she was wearing those tight black pants."

"You'd look good in those pants." He waggled his brows.

She playfully hit him, but truthfully thought it'd be fun to wear pants like that and saunter around like a sex kitten. She jumped off of the fence, extending her free hand to him. He intertwined his fingers with hers and walked with her toward her house.

"I'm surprised you even noticed," she said. The more she thought about it, the more she got jealous. Over Olivia Newton-

John. Who Finch would never meet, but still. It's the fact that he looked at her. Jeez, she felt pathetic. "You kept sighing and rolling your eyes throughout the movie."

"It's a musical."

"So?"

"So, people don't go around singing like that unless they're high or crazy. It's just unrealistic."

"And *Jaws* is?"

"Totally." He grinned and pushed the screen door open.

Katie and Preston's eyes darted to Evie, and they stopped speaking.

Silence.

"Did we interrupt something?" Evie asked. Because it sure looked like they had, she thought. Katie looked like a deer caught in headlights, and Preston had a look, Evie couldn't quite grasp what that look was, but it didn't feel right.

He got up and gave them a fake smile. "You put that salve on your feet every night and that should help the swelling."

"You're leaving?" Evie asked, gazing at Katie.

"I got an early start tomorrow." He took a quick look at Katie and added, "I'd better be going."

"You're not staying for supper?" Evie asked him. "Katie is a great cook."

He laughed. "I know. I've had the pleasure of eating her food, remember? I can't, Evie. I have plans."

"A date?" Evie pressed. That was curt, and Katie's scowl told her it was, but so help her, if Finch was right and he was up to no good, then she'd let him have it.

He laughed nervously. "You writing a book?"

"Maybe," she said and folded her arms against her chest. Waiting. Just waiting for him to slip. To fess up.

Finch wrapped his arms around Evie and gave her a little nudge, the kind that told her to keep her trap shut.

"She's got several chapters about me," Finch said, trying to lighten up that stiff room.

"I bet," Preston said with a wide grin. "See y'all soon." He shot out the door quicker than a fox being chased by hound dogs.

"Way to go, Eves!" Katie slammed her fist against the table.

"I didn't mean…" Evie's voice trailed off. Now she felt awful.

"Well, you did, and now he'll think I'm some love struck desperate pregnant woman trying to snatch him!"

"I just want to know where it's headed," Evie defended.

"You want to know where it's headed? Nowhere. He just came by to bring the salve and is enough of a gentleman to give me the time of day." She let out a grunt. "Oh, just let me be." She stormed off. Her hard footsteps pressed against the wood floors as she clambered up the steps.

Evie brought her hand to her mouth and stared at the empty space, wide-eyed.

"He didn't answer me," she said. "About the date."

"Maybe you should stay out of it."

"She's my best friend. I'm not going to stay out of it."

***

The phone rang. The sun had barely risen. Evie tripped over a pair of shoes and cursed. Finch always got on to her for leaving her shoes all over the floor.

"They belong in the closet," he'd say, and she'd brush him off, making him feel like he was crazy for bringing up such a notion.

Sore toed and nearly blind from the darkness, Evie ambled her way downstairs and picked the phone up to answer. "Hello." Her voice croaked, and her eye lids were half-closed.

"Evie, this is Ted Holt."

"Yes?" she said, wondering why in the world Holt was calling her before the rooster crowed. "Hi, Mr. Holt." Her voice perked up some, and her eyelids weren't as heavy but she still managed to yawn into the phone.

Finch tapped her on the shoulder, mouthing, "Who is it?"

"Our neighbor, Holt," she mouthed back, staring down at Finch's bare chest. She widened her eyes and ran a few fingers across the patch of hair on his chest.

He swooped her fingers away and shook his head, the way a parent would when they caught their kid's hand in the cookie jar.

"Evie, I don't know how to tell you this…" Holt started.

Her smile faded, and her knees wobbled. She sat down, knowing whatever it was, it wasn't good. News that began with that line was never good: "I don't know how to tell you this, but I'm pregnant. I don't know how to tell you this, but I'm leaving." Statements like those always began with that line and they always included a "but."

Finch sat next to her, staring at her peculiarly.

"I didn't see him. I didn't," he cried into the phone.

"Who?" Her heart stopped, or at least it felt like it did. She forgot to breathe.

No answer. Sobbing on the other end.

"Who?" she repeated with struggled breath. The waves were pounding her, crushing her. Who could it be? Dammit all, just when things were getting back to normal.

"It was…" He inhaled. "That pet ox of yours." He exhaled.

"Don't know what he was doing on my property. I was backing my truck up and..."

She threw the phone down. Holt's voice was on the other end still stuttering, saying "I'm sorry. I just hit him..."

She dashed outside.

"Miles!" she screamed. "Miles!" She scanned the property, high and low. Searching for a ghost. She ran all over the farm.

Holt had the wrong ox, she thought. He was mistaken. Miles never left the property. Never, and even though Holt lived nearby, there was no way Miles would ever make the trip. That's what Gray always said, "He was too smart to wander off."

"Miles!" she screamed over and over. Louder and louder until her voice was hoarse, and her vocal chords were strained. The sounds of her cries echoed in the dewey air.

Finch frantically ran to her.

"Evie," he breathed, talking the way hostage negotiators spoke before the swat team came in and did their business. He frowned at her and ran his fingers through her tousled hair. "He's..."

"Shh," she said, holding her index finger up and glaring at him. "Don't say it!"

He blinked back some tears and shook his head. "Miles is dead."

She thew her arms up in the air, pacing back and forth. "I don't believe you. You have to help me find him." Her blue eyes wide with frenzy and her voice was shaky and uneven.

Finch could work his magic. She always said he had a way with animals, and Miles loved him. He loved Finch. "He won't come. You call him, Finch. Make him come."

He placed his hands firmly on her shoulders. "Evie," he said, and by his tone and facial expression, she knew, she knew it was true.

But denying it was easier than accepting it.

"Miles!" she called. "Call him, dammit," she screamed at Finch. "Call him!" she punched at his chest, and he pulled her hands away from him and held her tight, encasing her small body into his.

"I'm so sorry, Evie," he murmured. "I'm so sorry."

CHAPTER 8

No one was able to explain how Miles, who had never left the property in all of the eight years of living there, ended up on Ted Holt's property early in the morning. Sure Holt lived next door. Evie's farm was nestled between Holt's property and the Myers' property. Holt was the preferred neighbor as the Myers boy was a pain in the ass, at least Finch thought he was since he was harassed by the pimply-faced brat.

No one could explain what compelled the docile ox to wander about. Whatever the case, Holt felt awful and apologized profusely. His wife sent over a care package, but Evie, she was still grieving. She'd never admit to it, but Finch saw the hurt in her eyes. Miles was the last reminder of her daddy, besides the house, the truck, and the land. Losing Miles was like losing her daddy all over again.

Evie insisted on having a funeral for Miles, and even though they thought it was peculiar to have a ceremony for an ox, they honored her wishes and went all out. Doris sang a bluesy rendition of "Amazing Grace," and Friedrich read a poem. Finch bought peonies and planted them at Miles' grave. He'd made a wooden hand-carved sign. Mouse played a tune on his harmonica, and Katie prepared a special meal. All of them contributed in some way, trying their darnedest to cheer her up.

"You should take her out for a special date," Doris suggested. "Women like being spoiled."

Friedrich nodded in agreement. "Take her out of this town. Go to a restaurant where the napkins are linen and chamber music is played."

"And food you can't pronounce," Doris added. "Make sure you

take her to one of those places where they speak French."

So Finch made plans. Big lofty plans to woo his woman, at least that's what he thought he was doing, wooing or courting or dating like gentleman did, what he thought a gentleman, the kind worthy of someone like Evie, would do.

He knew very little about high-class dining: which fork to use or what that one spoon was for. Katie knew a thing or two and tried to instruct him as best as she could. "My brain is mush, Finch," she said. "Since I got pregnant I can't think right." But she helped him as well as she could, enough so he wouldn't look like a jackhole when they sat down for dinner. He'd at least know what utensil to use.

He got dressed at the other house, wearing his Sunday best. All glossed up, his shirt was pressed and his shoes were polished. He spritzed on some of Friedrich's cologne and took a good hard look at himself in the mirror. Not bad, he thought. Not bad at all.

"Don't get cocky," Doris said, noticing his smug look. "Now go on and get out of here." She shooed him away, like a horsefly dancing around a plate of food.

"I still think it's kinda silly I'm getting dressed over here," he said on his way out the door.

"That's what makes it all the more romantic. Like a genuine date," Doris said with a girly laugh. "I make him do this from time to time." She side-glanced at Friedrich.

"It's true," Friedrich said.

"It spices things up." She gave a mischievous grin. "Course y'all are young so you don't need much spice, but when you're our age you will."

"I just hope this goes well." A wrinkle formed at the bridge of his nose. "This is a very important date."

Doris cupped his chin, and Finch swatted her hand away. He wasn't much for touching, unless it was Evie of course. Then he was all for it. "This will definitely cheer her up." She waggled her thin brows and grinned. "I'm happy as a clam, and I'm not the one going on the date." She giggled.

Finch's lips curled up, and he left Doris and Friedrich to their own devices. Mouse was sitting on a lawn chair, watching the sun set and enjoying the night. He whistled and hooted and hollered. "You almost look smart," he said.

"You, too." Finch formed a wry grin as he got into Evie's truck.

"Push her chair in when you sit down," Mouse shouted over the revving of the engine.

Finch gave him a quick nod to tell him he'd heard him, but he knew enough to push her chair in, hold her door open for her, watch his mouth around her, things like that, things he'd picked up along the way. Gestures his mom, Friedrich and Rolf had taught him as he grew up. Doris would have liked to take credit for teaching him how to be a gentleman, but truth be told she'd only influenced him a smidgen. It was Friedrich who really taught him how to be treat a woman. The man loved women and not in a sick perverted chauvinistic way, but the way you could tell that he respected them, thought they were God's gift and should be cherished as such.

Finch had cleaned the truck and used some of that deodorizer that Mike used when he finished working on the cars. The entire truck smelled like fabric softener. He figured that was better than its usual smell: o'd manure. Sometimes he'd be working on cars in Mike's garage and swear he smelled cow poop. Mike would just laugh and tell him that it was burned into those nostrils of his.

And he'd even gone to the trouble of vacuuming the floorboards, although, so much of the dirt and other particles he couldn't identify had seeped so deeply into the carpet that the full force power of a vacuum didn't even make a dent.

He had shaved his face, just minutes before, and Friedrich's aftershave still stung. God he felt like an ass. He stared at himself in the mirror to make sure he looked all right. Evie knew what he looked like, and she didn't seem to have a problem with it. But tonight, he was just so darn antsy. Squirmy even.

He was at the front door, holding a bouquet of peonies, her favorite, and waiting, waiting to knock on the door to the house where he now lived. The whole thing seemed ridiculous, but Doris said, hell, everyone said, it'd do the trick. It'd be the most romantic date Evie would never forget. That's what he wanted, a night to remember, like those lame prom themes kids used when they couldn't come up with anything better. He just wanted this night to become a memory for her. The kind she'd think about when she was sitting on the front porch swing swaying with the wind on a warm summer's day, sipping on sweet tea and thinking about her life. He wanted this to be a memory she saw vividly when she was too old to remember what day it was but she could recount detail for detail what this night was for her.

He tapped on the door, and Katie opened it, beaming, then she started to cry.

"Don't," Finch said. He'd seen the floodgates open from her more than enough in the past few months. The more pregnant she got, the more she cried. He'd heard her crying after hearing John Denver's *Annie's Song*.

"It's so romantic," she had said, and Finch had to restrain himself from rolling his eyes at her. He'd been around plenty of pregnant women on the circuit, and one thing he learned, keep your mouth shut and nod like it's all normal. Otherwise, you'll face a terrible wrath: a pregnant woman's anger was ten times—no a hundred times—worse than anyone else's.

She sniffled. "You look good."

"Thanks," he said. He felt good. He felt like a thousand bucks actually.

He scanned the room.

"She's coming down in a minute," Katie said. "I think this is romantic. What you're doing."

Finch shrugged. Women. Give a girl some wildflowers, and she'd think you hung the moon. Take her out on a date and you're a hero. Sometimes the opposite sex confused the hell out of him. Well, not sometimes, most of the time.

"She's been giddy as a girl on her wedding day," Katie continued. "Y'all haven't been on a date in a long time."

What was last week, Finch thought. He'd taken her to The Diner and they shared spaghetti like in *Lady and The Tramp* because Evie thought it'd be fun. But the noodles were greasy, and the sauce was watered down. Italian food wasn't the specialty at The Diner.

Women, he thought. So all of those times they'd gone out in the past few months didn't count as dates? Because he didn't drive to the house and pick her up like he was doing right there and then? Women.

Evie came down the stairs, and Finch's brown eyes stuck to her like concrete. God, she was beautiful. She wore a red strapless dress and those platform shoes of hers he liked so much, like those women dancing in *Saturday Night Fever*. He cleared his throat, swallowed, cleared his throat again. His heart beat faster, too fast for a man his age, and his palms were starting to dampen.

Her blonde hair was feathered. He got a whiff of her from the bottom of the steps. What was that scent? It was like a fresh floral bouquet. He inhaled and thought, I could kiss that neck of hers for hours.

She took the flowers from his hands and smiled: a big, wide grin. The lovestruck kind that made him warm inside. The kind that told him he'd done good.

She put them in a vase, and Katie said, taking them out of her hands, "I'll go put some water in this. Y'all have fun." She scooted out of the room, giving them some privacy, which Finch thought was ironic since they all lived together. What'd they need privacy for? But this night, it was different. It was like going on a first date with her all over again.

"You look nice," she told him. She scanned him up and down, like he was eye candy, and fiddled with his hair, brushing his bangs away from his eyes. "Real nice," she added quietly.

He felt the heat rush to his cheeks. He was blushing, like a stupid school boy.

"Thanks," he said, clearing his throat. "You look really pretty."

She stepped back, wide-mouthed and wide-eyed. "Finch Mills. I think that is the first time you've ever said that to me."

"Don't let it go to your head," he teased. Maybe he hadn't ever said it out loud. But he'd thought it. Every single day of his life since he'd met her. He'd thought it. She was a supernova. The stars. The moon and the sky. She was magnificent.

"Ready?" he asked.

She nodded, still awe struck by his compliment, and grabbed her clutch. They headed out the door.

***

"You're taking me across the state line," she said as they passed a sign that read "Welcome to North Carolina."

He side-glanced her and smiled.

"Where are we going?" she asked.

"That's a secret," he said and fiddled with the radio. The further they went away from Haines, the worse the signal. "We've Only Just Begun" by the Carpenters was barely audible. Karen Carpenter's voice faded in and out, with only a few lyrics emitting.

"I'm surprised you didn't blindfold me," she said.

"I like your blue eyes too much to do that."

"Yours will do I guess," she teased.

After driving for close to an hour, he drove down a narrow gravel road in the middle of the forest. Bouchon was situated near a mountain lake and out far enough that when you went there to dine, you stayed a while.

"We're out in the sticks," Evie said, and Finch laughed. Haines was in the sticks. Sure, Bouchon was in a remote location, but it was near a big enough town that he saw a Dairy Dream on the way in. Even Haines didn't have a Dairy Dream.

He jumped out of the truck and rushed to get her door, offering her his hand to help her get down.

Lights illuminated the brick path that led to the wooden structure. A terrace faced the lake and symphonic music played.

"How pretty," Evie said.

Finch breathed a sigh of relief. It had taken him some time to find this place. Katie had told him about it, and he had to sleuth his way through the Yellow Pages to get the telephone number and make reservations.

He opened the front door, and they were greeted by the maitre d', a middled-aged man wearing a tuxedo.

"My, my, this is spiffy," she said, peering down at her dress, brushing her hands along the fabric to ensure there weren't any wrinkles as a result of their long ride. "Glad I painted my nails."

"Because if you hadn't, they'd kick us out," he whispered and pinched her hip. He loved her hips. And her legs. And her face. And her lips. Okay, everything about her. He would rest his hand on her hip the entire night if she'd let him.

"Yes, may I help you?" the maitre d' did a once over, scanning them up and down and hardening his stare to Finch.

"We have reservations for Mills," Finch said.

The maitre d' checked his book and looked back up at them. "Yes, we have your name here, Mr. Mills. We have a jacket you can wear if you don't have one."

A jacket? For what, Finch thought. He had his denim jacket in the truck.

"It's required," he explained as if reading Finch's mind. "I'll be right back." He went to another room.

"I don't think he's bringing back a denim jacket," Evie teased.

He approached them, holding an avocado green jacket with yellow pin-striping. Good God, it was hideous. Finch wasn't much for fashion, but even he knew that piece of crap was just that: a piece of crap.

The maitre d' gestured for Finch to open up his arms and then put the jacket on Finch.

It was tight. And stank. Like old man.

Finch felt stupid and awkward and not handsome like he had earlier. Now he was just a big tool.

"Follow me," the maitre d' said.

They made their way through a maze of tables and chairs. The lighting was dim, but from what Finch could see, old people congregated there: blue-haired women and white-haired men who wore ascots. And given the jewelry that sparkled around the women's sagging necks and pruned wrists, they had money. Lots and lots of it.

The maitre d' scooted Evie's chair in for her before Finch had time to do it and handed them menus.

Evie's eyes widened. "Good Lord, Finch, did you see the price for a glass of wine?"

He scanned the menu. Holy crap on a stick! One glass of wine was the equivalent of ten milkshakes at Dairy Dream.

"What made you choose this place?" Evie said.

"Katie recommended it. She said she and Todd went here for prom." He was starting to think that listening to Katie wasn't always the best idea. He felt his wallet, checking on the stash of bills he had in it. They'd have to scrimp: no dessert and no drinks, but he could manage.

A waiter approached their table and asked them both what they wanted to drink. Each said water, and he left, clicking on his heels.

Evie's brow wrinkled, and her nose did that crinkly thing that Finch thought was so cute.

"What?" he asked. He already mucked the date up. What a tool, indeed. The place was stodgy and the jacket itched. He figured it was wool, and it smelled starchy.

"Finch, there's stuff on here I can't pronounce, and it's..." she leaned forward and turned side-to-side before she whispered, "really expensive."

He placed his hand on hers and said, "It's okay." He'd break the bank for her.

"We don't have to eat here."

"It's fine."

"No, I'm serious."

"I wanted to treat you to a nice date."

"Finch, I don't need all of this. I'm fine eating a hamburger and drinking a milk shake. Let's get out of here," she said and giggled. "There was a Dairy Dream on the way in. We'll make a run for it before he comes back with our water. I bet they charge for that too."

"You sure?"

She nodded and turned her head side to side before she stood up. "Come on." She speed walked out of there before Finch had a chance to respond. She kept her head low with her eyes focused on the front door.

Finch quickened his pace and pushed the door open. As soon as they reached the outside, they let out a whopper of a laugh. The kind you got from watching a good sitcom.

Finch glanced down and saw that he was still wearing that awful suit jacket. "I left it on," he complained.

"You can't go back in there."

"Well, I can't steal it either. Not that I'd want to." He thought for a moment, then took the jacket off and wrapped it around the hay-filled scarecrow's body, which was a part of the autumn décor.

"Poor scarecrow. He looks like a tacky hobo now," Evie said, and they made a dash for the truck as the restaurant's front door opened.

***

It was a clear night. The stars shined, and the air was crisp and cool. As the wind gently blew, leaves from trees found their way to the ground, trickling down one by one. Finch and Evie sat in the truck bed, slurping on their milkshakes and munching on their cheeseburgers.

She kicked her legs back and forth and smiled. "This is the best date ever."

"Really?"

"Of course." She held his hand.

They had parked the truck off in an empty field with nothing but the country around them. Finch was glad he'd remembered to stash a blanket in the truck. It was a brisk night, and Evie hadn't thought to bring a jacket. He had wrapped the blanket around her the moment they sat down, making sure she was snug and warm. His denim jacket would do for the night. Wouldn't do for Bouchon, but it'd do for the outdoors.

"Best hamburger ever," she said.

He patted his full belly. "It was good."

She intertwined her fingers with his. "This is so much better than that restaurant. I swear I saw someone eating snails when we walked in." She smacked her lips in disgust.

"I tried," he said softly, sighing.

"You don't have to try with me, you know? This right here is perfect."

Elton John's "Your Song" began to play on the truck's radio. Finch jumped off of the truck bed and offered Evie his hand. "Want to dance?"

Her eyes darted back and forth. "Here?"

"Yep."

He wrapped his hands around her waist, enjoying his fingers grazing against her hips. He set her down on the grass and pulled her close to him. She waited for him to take the lead.

Finch lifted her arms up, brought them around his neck and placed his hands back on her hips. He swayed side to side, and Evie followed. As Elton John sang about love, Finch brought Evie closer to him. She lay her head against his chest and formed a soft smile of satisfaction. If this was what being in love was all about, she understood why so many people wrote beautiful, heartfelt songs about it.

He leaned down to kiss her, tasting vanilla and sweetness, because that's what Evie was: sweet as apple pie and all things good. He closed his eyes, enjoying that moment. That incredible moment of knowing that luck had finally walked into his life.

Evie was a forever type of girl. Not a passing fling. Not a halfway point in a man's life. She was permanence. She was what Finch saw when he pictured his own mortality. She was his forever.

***

"Why are you parking here?" Evie asked. The truck idled on the dirt road behind Evie's house. It was near the pond and on the far end of the property.

He twitched his brows. "Just follow me." He turned the engine off and grabbed her hand as she slid across the truck seat and exited the driver's side. He gazed down at her and said, "Your shoes will get dirty." It had rained the day before, and the ground was still soft. He pointed to his back and said, "Get on."

Evie jumped on him and giggled as Finch carried her piggy-back style to the pond.

"What are you up to?" she asked as he set her down. She couldn't stop laughing. The rush. The feeling. Just being with him on this night made her giddy.

The front of Gray's old row boat rested on the shore of the pond as the water lapped it back and forth. "I thought we'd go out on the pond."

"At night?"

"Yeah," he answered, like Evie was crazy for even suggesting that it was the wrong time of day to venture out in the pond in an old row boat.

"Okay?" she questioned.

He extended his hand to Evie and helped her get in the boat. She sat on the wooden bench and gripped onto the sides of the boat.

Finch took off his shoes and tossed them in the boat. He rolled up his pants. "Whew."

A few goosebumps formed as he made his way through the murky frigid water. He hopped in and paddled away from shore.

"Cold, isn't it?" Evie said, noticing he was gritting his teeth.

"It's fine," he lied.

She folded her arms against her chest and narrowed her eyes to his. She couldn't see his reaction. The moon was half full, and it was too dark to get a good look at him. He handed her a blanket, and she wrapped it around her, just waiting. Waiting to see what he was up to taking her out in the middle of the pond at night.

"Nice night, isn't it?" he said. She heard him breathing all heavy. The exertion of paddling was getting to him. Her daddy only had one paddle. What was Finch thinking, she thought. She hadn't been out in that boat since the other paddle got lost and was probably down on the bottom of that pond rotting away.

Lights flickered in the distance, and Evie leaned forward. "What's that?" There was an edge to her voice, and her heart was racing. Fast.

"Nothing."

She pointed. "I think I see people." She shook the boat as she shifted on the bench. "There's people over there, Finch!" she whispered loudly. Her fingers dug into his knees in a fit of nerves.

He laid the paddle down in the boat and let it float with the breeze. "It's okay." He patted her on the hands, gently removing each and every one of her glued fingers from his sore knees.

The lights moved with the shadowy figures behind them. "We need to go see who it is," she said and picked up the paddle.

She held onto the paddle and moved it in the water—back and forth—but she wasn't going anywhere. Her breath was hard and heavy. She was using every ounce she had in her just to move an inch or two. "Good Lord, Finch. We're not moving."

"Evie, put the paddle down."

She gave him a strange look and dropped it. "What is wrong with you tonight?" She jerked her head and got real quiet. "There's music. I hear David Bowie. Is that Bowie?" she asked him.

She swore she saw signs. Big signs. With words written on them. She inched closer, so close to Finch, and breathed into him, nearly sitting on top of him. She squinted. "There are signs. Look over there." She pointed, but Finch's eyes were stuck on hers.

He moved her hair and kissed her neck, grazing it with his lips.

She shoved him away. "This isn't the time for that. What is going on?" she asked in frustration.

He laughed, and she inched back. "I can't read them." She

opened her mouth and screamed, "It's on fire! It's on fire!"

Finch turned to look.

A blaze of fire and frenzied voices filled the night air. Finch let out a heavy sigh and started to paddle, but the boat wasn't cooperating.

"What the hell?" she said, trying to get something out of Finch, but he was cursing under his breath, jerking on that paddle with all of his might.

She stared down at her feet in horror. A puddle of water had formed and was getting larger by the second.

"Finch!" She screamed, pointing down.

He looked down, then up at her. His face was stricken with the same look of panic as hers. "There's a leak."

They searched the boat for the hole, and Evie found it. Too wide to plug with a finger, she covered it with one hand and scooped water out with her other. "We've gotta get out of here!"

Finch paddled like there was no tomorrow as water crept in like the Angel of Death. "It's filling up fast," she said. "We're going to sink."

She scooped water out as Finch paddled as fast as he could, but there was too much water. It reached Finch's ankles and Evie's calves. The hem of her dress was drenched. "We're going to have to swim back," she said.

"But it's cold."

She jumped from the boat and into the pond, screeching when her body was submerged into the cold water.

Finch tossed the paddle, cursed at the damn boat and joined Evie.

Their teeth chattered as they treaded water. "Brr..." Evie said, her teeth clattering, and they started swimming to the shore. "Thisss was a greattt idea."

He decided not to retort.

Evie followed Finch out of the pond and saw Doris, Friedrich, Mouse and Katie stomping all over the embers, trying to get the fire out. The sign was scorched. Three other signs laid on the ground, and as Evie moved closer and got a better look, she saw the words: Will. You. Me?

"Will you me," she repeated. "Will you me, what?"

Evie shivered violently. Her red dress stuck to her cold skin. Finch rubbed her arms, but his wet hands were no source of comfort.

"Y'all better go warm up or you're gonna lose a toe or two," Doris shouted.

"Sorry we messed this up," Friedrich said.

"We?" Mouse scoffed. "Who held the lantern too close to their sign?" He darted his eyes in Friedrich's direction.

Friedrich gave a nervous laugh and looked down at the ground.

"Want me to put the song back on?" Katie offered to Finch and waddled to the portable record player.

Finch rubbed his arms, and his body slightly shook. He complained under his breath as David Bowie's voice echoed into the night air.

"What?" Evie shivered. "Is going on?"

"I wanted it," Finch said with a shaky voice. "To be perfect."

"What, Finch? What?" she asked. She wiped droplets of water away from her eyes and wrung out the bottom of her dress.

"Just do it already, Finch," Doris hollered.

He breathed hard and reached down into his pant pocket. He

pulled out a small square box and held it in the palm of his hand.

Evie's blue eyes widened and then darted back to the scorched sign. David Bowie's song, "Be My Wife" played. She smiled. Wide and gushy. The lightbulb was on. Now she got what he was up to. Now it all made sense.

"It was going to be perfect for you, but now it's just a mess," he said with a frown. He kicked the dirt and sighed.

"It's only a mess if you don't follow through with your plans," she said.

She felt her heart pounding against her chest. She knew what was coming, and her ears were ringing, maybe from the cold pond water, but they were ringing, waiting for his voice to utter four words to her because she had dreamed about this for weeks and weeks and weeks.

"Ask her," Doris said.

"Don't be a milquetoast," Friedrich added.

"Get on your knees," Mouse said, and Katie laughed.

Finch rolled his eyes at them.

Evie brought her hands to her face, making sure she was alive and breathing and this wasn't a dream. She watched as Finch stood before her, his brown eyes earnest and sincere. She took a mental snapshot of him, wanting to replay this memory for years to come.

"Evie, I love you," he said. " And I want forever with you." He cleared his throat. "Will you be my wife?"

She leapt onto him and wrapped her legs around his waist. She kissed him on his cheeks, his neck, his forehead, and finally his lips.

"Ahem," Doris said. "Quit swapping spit and give him an answer."

"Yes! Of course! Yes!" Evie screeched, and everyone clapped.

Hoots and hollers. Whistles and offers of congratulations. The air was buzzing with happiness.

Finch kissed Evie and whispered in her ear, "Mrs. Mills has a nice ring to it, doesn't it?"

Evie nodded and let out a laugh. "And I say the sooner it changes the better."

"Well, what's stopping us?" he said.

***

Evie lay in bed staring at her left ring finger. The marquise diamond sparkled from the morning sun, creating a spectrum of colors painting the white ceiling. It had been Rolf's mother's ring, and according to Finch, he'd gotten it from Rolf when they went to Gibsonton.

"Rolf didn't mind parting with this?" she had asked.

Finch shrugged. "I'm really the only family he has. I mean we're not related by blood, but he's like a grandfather to me."

"It's gorgeous," she had said, thinking for a moment. "So this whole time you've had the ring knowing you were going to ask me?"

"Yep," he had said with a smug expression.

He played with her hair while she lay her head in his lap.

"And you waited this long to ask me?" she said.

"I wanted it to be perfect," he admitted. She saw his Adam's apple move as he swallowed.

She began to laugh, thinking how his idea of perfect became a real debacle.

"What's so funny?" he asked.

"All of it." She laughed again. "The boat sinking." She chortled. "The sign lighting on fire."

He reached down and started to tickle her under the arms. "I'm glad you think it's so funny."

"Not the arms," she whined, scooting away. He trapped her with his arms and rolled on top of her. He lay there, staring down at her, and he leaned down to kiss her gently on the lips before he rolled off of her.

They had stayed up talking, discussing places they wanted to go for their honeymoon even though they knew some of those places were just pipe dreams. Places they'd never go because life was in the way.

Evie peeked at Finch. He was sound asleep or at least he was acting like he was. She couldn't tell. She waved her hand in front of his closed eyes, and he didn't flinch. Just as she was about to get out of bed, he pulled her by the waist and smiled at her with one eye open.

"Finch!" She giggled.

She rolled on top of him, and he ran his fingers through her fallen hair, tugging it behind her ears. "Let's get our marriage license today," he said.

"Finch Mills, I think you finally had a brilliant idea." She teased, thinking that this was her perfect, and nothing was going to tarnish it. Nothing.

CHAPTER 9

Evie sat in the kitchen eating lunch with Katie. It had been difficult getting through the morning. Evie thought about nothing but going with Finch to the courthouse to apply for a marriage license. He said he'd ask for the afternoon off, and then they'd go. The sooner they applied, the better. She didn't need a huge, over-the-top type of wedding. She was fine standing under that big shade tree near the pond and having her closest friends and family witnessing them as they said their "I do's."

Katie couldn't stop beaming. "Good Lord, Katie, you'd think you were the one getting married," Evie said.

"I can't help it, Eves. He's a catch, and y'all are so in love." Her stomach had expanded and touched the edge of the table even though she sat a good half a foot away from it. Evie was worried that Katie wouldn't handle it well – her getting married while she was pregnant by a man who'd flown the coop once a baby was conceived.

"And how'd you keep quiet about it?" Evie asked. It shocked her to discover that they all knew before she did: Mouse, Friedrich, Doris, and Katie.

Katie shrugged. "He didn't tell me until a day before, so I didn't have to keep it secret for long."

"For you that's a long time." Since they'd been best friends, Evie knew from previous experiences that Katie was an open book and would confess to anything under pressure. She never knew Katie had a poker face and wondered what other secrets she was hiding from her.

"You never asked, so I didn't have to tell," Katie explained.

"Ahh, so I should have pointed a flash light at you and asked you until you fessed up," Evie teased.

"I still wouldn't have said anything."

"Sure you wouldn't have. I bet Finch didn't tell you till the last minute."

"No." Katie folded her arms against her stomach and huffed. "We all knew, and you're just sore 'cause you found out last."

Evie didn't respond. She wasn't sore; she was just surprised she hadn't caught on since Finch had been acting weird that entire day. But sometimes she was so wrapped up in the farm and those cows that she let things slip and told herself she'd think about them later. Sometimes later became never, and lately, all she thought about was those cows and if this was what life had intended for her: to do nothing but raise cows. She'd given some deep thought to what Finch had mentioned – working with Tom, her vet. She knew he needed the help, and half the time he'd say, "Evie, you know more than I do about these here cows." And sometimes that was true. If anything, her daddy knew cows like the back of his hand, and every sixth sense she got about cattle was a result of her DNA. She brushed the thought away and figured she'd think about it later.

"Have you heard from Preston?" Evie asked. She'd been curious about the two of them, and Katie didn't divulge a peep, which was odd for Katie. When she and Todd dated, Evie got an ear full about their love life, often enough to cause Evie's stomach to churn because it seemed all they did was make-out and then some. She thought Todd was a scumbag and never understood how Katie could have liked him well enough to have a baby with him. Love was blind, and in this case it was cataracts, glaucoma, and Stevie Wonder all rolled into one.

Katie clammed up and twisted her hands and arms together like a pretzel. Her face became flushed. "No."

Evie couldn't read her. And she was so darn antsy with her answer, like a jitter bug. She cocked a brow, watching as her best friend shot up from the table and poured more tea.

"I thought maybe something was brewing between you two," Evie pressed.

Katie sighed heavily. "Who wants an unmarried pregnant woman, Eves?"

"You're a catch."

Katie gave her a look and then frowned. "Let's see, I'm homeless, unmarried, and pregnant. Yeah, I'd say that was enough to make any man drop everything and marry me."

Evie didn't know what to say and opened her mouth but hesitated, reading the look of hurt in Katie's eyes.

She dabbed at her hazel eyes and said in a low quiet voice, "I'm fat as a whale. I miss seeing my feet, you know that? And I've got nothin'."

"You have us," Evie said.

"I know, and I love y'all, but he," she peered down at her stomach, "is all I have. I don't have a cent to my name, and he's coming in the world with grandparents who want nothing to do with him, and a father who'd rather sleep around and party it up instead of being there for him."

"They're all stupid," Evie blurted and then regretted it. That wasn't the time to discuss their intelligence levels or to say such a thing. It didn't sound sympathetic. "I'm sorry," she added quietly.

Katie let out a laugh. "Especially Todd. You know, I ran into his mom when I was downtown the other day?"

Evie leaned in.

"And she acted like she couldn't see me, even though I was standing a few feet away from her saying her name. She just kept on walking, talking to her stuck up friend who didn't mind giving me the evil eye. Like I'm some hussy who tainted their perfect son," Katie said.

"I always thought his mom was dumb."

"Dumb enough that she says 'bobbed wire' instead of 'barbed wire,'" she said and giggled. "I heard her mispronounce it so many times, I was tempted to ask her who was this Bob and why was he on a wire."

"He's that old guy that sells wire down the road." Evie snickered.

Katie wiped her eyes and smiled. "I appreciate all you've done for me, and I'll never be able to repay you."

"Who cares about that?"

"I wish I could," she grew quiet for a moment. "Eves, I'm really scared," she confided.

"I know, but you'll be okay," Evie said with a confident nod and went to hug her. "You've got this," she added. "I believe in you."

Katie slowly got up and said, "Well, I guess I'm gonna finish cleaning up."

"There isn't anything to clean."

"It gives me something to do, makes me feel like I'm useful," Katie said, and for that, Evie felt like a big fat heel.

Katie walked out of the kitchen. Evie noticed the dust rag and polish sitting on the table, and she grabbed it and called out to Katie from the kitchen as she made her way to the living room. "Katie!"

"Ka..." she stopped mid-sentence, gobsmacked and speechless, staring at the person standing behind the screen door. Her feet became dead weights, and her body had just given up, like it went on vacation and said, "see ya later."

Katie was just standing there, making the same face as Evie. She was uttering something. Evie couldn't hear her. Her ears were ringing, and her blood was boiling. Hot. Her heart was amped up: BOOM. BOOM. BOOM. She sucked in air and tried to breathe right but her body felt constricted, like someone was slowly crushing her with weights.

Evie flared her nostrils and balled her hands into fists. "What the hell are you doing here?" she snapped.

***

Finch was on top of the world. He felt like his life was a Carpenters' song, all cheery and rosy-cheeks with a promise of good things to come. He was surprised he hadn't skipped his way into Mike's shop. He was getting married. To Evie. The love of his life, and nothing was going to stand in his way. All he wanted was a normal life, a place to all home, and a person to spend time with.

The radio wasn't blaring like usual. Usually Finch would enter the garage with 1950s music playing on Mike's cruddy radio. Mike wasn't working on a car either. Most days, Finch would find Mike's feet under a car and nudge him with his, saying "Hello."

Mike was pacing around the shop. He was muttering to himself and fidgeting with a wrench.

"Hey," Finch said. "I have something to tell you!" He was beaming, like a doofus, but he couldn't stop the happiness from filling him. Who cared if he looked like a tool? He was too damn happy to care.

Mike formed a wry face. "I need to talk to you."

The news could wait, Finch thought. Whatever Mike had to tell him, it wasn't going to be good. He knew by Mike's expression and the way he couldn't make direct eye contact.

Mike gestured to his stools and they both sat, facing each other. Mike sat for a second and got up. He rubbed his face. Grease stains latched onto his sweaty skin. He took off his cap and ran his fingers through his dirty hair. He sat back down for a moment, then shot right back up, all the time mumbling to himself.

"Settle down, Mike," Finch said. He was like a Yo-yo, going up and down, and it was making Finch sick.

"Sorry," he said, all flustered. "I like having you here, Finch."

"I like being here," Finch said with some hesitation.

"But people are talking, and I'm sure you've noticed business has slowed down."

Sure Finch had noticed. There were fewer cars coming in. Fewer customers. But he just assumed it was the nature of the business: one season they're swamped and the next they're not. The carnival was like that. One night they'd be packed, the next night they'd hear nothing but crickets chirping.

"I've gotten a lot of calls, and I've just been blowing them off. People in this town can be..." he struggled for the right word.

Finch could fill in the gap: Judgmental. Uppity. Nosy.

"Real opinionated," Mike decided.

Finch nodded. That was a good way to describe a lot of the locals.

"And, well, uh," he lowered his head for a moment and then looked back at Finch. Tears were forming in the man's eyes. Finch slumped on the stool and frowned, knowing the big blow was coming.

"They've threatened to take their business elsewhere unless I let you go," he said.

There it was, Finch thought. The words he'd been waiting for. A feeling of sadness filled him. Just minutes earlier he thought nothing could stand in his way. But now he was out of a job because some idiot townspeople didn't like him.

"I've lost some customers already, but yesterday, a big group of them came to my house and said they'd take their cars to Chester because they didn't want you working on them."

"Why?" Finch asked, even though he knew. He'd always be a carny to them.

"They're claiming that there's been some stealing, and they blame you for the accident at the carnival."

"I'm not a thief!" Finch shot up. "And you know damn well that I didn't cause that accident. It was Dmitri and Nate McDaniels." He hissed when he said his name. If someone asked Finch Mills who he hated with all of his might, he'd say Nate Fucking McDaniels.

Mike held up his palm and blinked. "I know. I know."

"Then why didn't you tell them that?"

"I tried, Finch. I sure tried, but they got their own mindset, and you see, a lot of them are the town elders and well, people listen to them. So, if they go around telling people you're opening their gates and letting cattle out and stealing their chickens, then people are likely to believe them."

Finch scoffed, "I'm not doing those things. How could they think that?"

"They think it's you and your friends because none of it was happening until y'all moved here. I know better, but they don't believe me," he said and moved close to Finch, tapping him on the shoulder. "And, 'cause you ain't from around here."

"So, because I'm an outsider I'm the cause of all of this?"

"Yes," Mike whispered.

It took everything Finch had in him not to flinch. Mike wasn't to blame. He was just a man trying to feed his family, and if the town was telling him they weren't going to frequent his business anymore, he'd have to do what he could to save it. Finch would do the same.

"It's okay," Finch said. But it wasn't. If the town hated him, how was this going to affect him and Evie?

Miked wiped at his eyes and said, "You're the best mechanic I've ever known."

"It's okay," Finch said, thinking how quickly the tables had turned. Now he was consoling Mike.

"It'll die down. They'll get over it soon, and I'll be able to bring you back," Mike said, but Finch knew that wasn't going to happen. Ignorance and hate went hand in hand, and if those people had decided they hated Finch, they'd hate him until the day they died.

"Yeah, sure," Finch lied. Was Evie better off without him? He'd already ruined her reputation. Now he was worthless. He couldn't even work in that godforsaken town.

"What were you going to tell me?" Mike asked.

"Nothing," Finch said. "It's nothing."

CHAPTER 10

"I said," she breathed hard and heavy, like an old woman who'd just walked up hill, "What the hell are you doing here?" She finally had the resolve to move, and her feet pounded against the wood floors as she made her way to the front door. "Well..." Evie continued, tapping her foot against the floor. Her arms folded tight across her chest and her chin jutted out. A screen door was all that separated them.

"You always had a temper, Evelyn," Rebecca Barnes said.

And like that, Evie grabbed onto the door handle and slammed the front door shut. She wiped her hands together and said, "That's, that."

"Eves," Katie said and swallowed.

Evie spewed curse words under her breath and paced. She threw her arms up in the air. "She's here now. What does she want? Money? 'Cause there isn't any!"

"I don't know, Eves. Maybe you should talk to her. She's your mother," Katie said quietly, as gentle as a lion tamer.

Evie shot her a look. "Talk to her? There's nothing worth talking about to *her*," she said with disdain.

Katie gave Evie a sympathetic look and was at a loss for words. She peeked out the front window and said, "She's not alone, Eves."

Evie stalked to the window and gasped. "Lawd have mercy."

***

Fired. He'd been fired. And for what? For things he hadn't done. For being a carny. He knew prejudice, he'd experienced it his entire life. But this? This affected his relationship with Evie.

He drove fast. He was so angry. Pissed even. Mad at the world.

Mad that ignorant people continued to sway others' beliefs—others' opinions, when that's what they were: opinions. These people didn't know jack squat about him or his friends. They didn't know the hearts that Mouse, Friedrich, and Doris had. And him? He'd never steal. He'd never harm a kid.

But they thought he would. And that was all that mattered. All it took was for one person to believe.

He punched the steering wheel and cursed. He shouted every expletive he could think of. Right when his life was on track. Just when he got a taste of normal.

He slammed on his brakes. Damn kids running out in the road like they owned it. After he caught his breath, he got a really good look at them: One boney-legged pimply-faced kid and his thin and gangly cronies ran into the woods, laughing like jackasses. Hee haw. Hee haw.

Finch heard a chicken squawking. He looked out the passenger side window and saw a hen tied to a fence post. He got out of the truck and went over to the chicken. Gently, he untied the sisal rope from around its thin legs and picked it up, holding it tight enough so it couldn't get away. The hen's wings fluttered, and it squawked loud.

He jetted to the truck and shut the door quickly. The hen flapped around in the cab, pecking at everything and anything: Finch's legs, the seat and the door. He made a quick turn and headed to the Holt's farm.

Finch parked the truck and scooped up the irritated hen. It pecked at his arms. He was sure to have marks where that pointed beak pierced his skin.

He didn't reach the front porch before Mr. Holt greeted him.

"Can I help you?" he asked Finch with an incredulous look. He spit chewing tobacco out of his mouth. A pile of saliva and brown liquid formed on his porch step.

"I was driving and saw your hen was tied to your fence post."

Mr. Holt took the hen from Finch's hands and held it still. His hand clamped around its mouth, and he pressed it under his arm like it was a football.

"Tied to my fence post, you say?" Holt made a face, the kind that said, I'm not buying what you're saying.

"Yes. I saw some kids running off. I think they may have done it."

"Kids will be kids, won't they? Well, thanks for your trouble," Holt said, still giving Finch a skeptical look. He did a once over on him, scanning him up and down. "You're that carny boy that's living next door with Gray's daughter, ain't you?"

"Yes," Finch said. "Finch Mills." He extended his hand.

"Humph," he muttered. "Living together when you ain't married ain't right, you know?"

Finch had just about had it with this town. With these people. With the entire day. He decided not to add fuel to the man's fire by responding with what he really was thinking, which was filled with insults and curse words sure to make anyone blush. Instead he settled for a safe phrase. "I better be going," he said and headed back to the truck with the chicken squawking and the man just telling it to shush while he drove off.

***

"She's the spittin' image..." Katie said.

"Don't say it," Evie interrupted, but even she had to agree with Katie. The blonde hair. The blue eyes. The same small nose. It was like looking in a mirror ten years ago.

Evie's eyes met her mother's, and they just stared at each other. Evie was getting a good look at the woman she hadn't seen in ten years. Ten whole years. That's how long it'd been since she had seen her, and now she was just a person. A stranger. Someone from her past.

"Eves, you think...?"

***

Finch banged on the door. He was as restless as a lovestruck fool in a romantic film, trying to square away his problems, place all of his ducks in one nice neat row, and squash his problems with the thud of his fist.

"Hold your horses," Doris said.

Finch bent over and caught his breath.

"Honey Lamb, you okay?"

He stood upright and gave her a solemn expression.

Friedrich and Mouse joined her at the door. "Come inside for a Coca Cola," Doris said and placed her hands on him.

Finch sat at the small round table with Mouse and Friedrich. Doris popped open a glass bottle of Coke and slid it his way. Finch took a long swig and gulped, thankful for the drink.

"What's ailing you, Honey Lamb?"

"I was fired," he blurted. Doris sat down next to him and patted him on the hand.

Friedrich frowned. "Why?"

"Why do you think?" Finch said, bitter, bitter sarcasm filled his core.

"Because of the carnival," Friedrich said with an exasperated sigh.

Finch told them the tale, how'd he been fired and why.

Mouse's lips curled down, and he said, "People make their own impressions. Like this house. It's not much for looking at on the outside, but inside it's warm and full of life. Most people don't look past the outside."

"This affects Evie and me," Finch said.

"This only affects you if you allow it to. Did you know that Doris' parents do not like me?" Friedrich said. "They told her they'd disown her if she married me because of my tattoos." He laughed. "As if tattoos make a man bad."

"But you aren't married?" Finch said.

"We're married in the eyes of common law, but that is not the point. If we had allowed them to stand in our way, I would've missed out on the best fifteen years of my life."

"Sixteen, but who's counting?" Doris chimed in. "And we sure didn't make them change their tunes when we decided not to marry. Daddy said I was livin' in sin with Friedrich and he couldn't stand for his daughter to shame him like that."

"You can't change these people's minds. This is their problem. Not yours. And not Evie's," Friedrich said.

"But my job? Her farm? It could be at risk," Finch said.

"You take that risk," Friedrich said. "Isn't that what really living means: taking risks?"

Finch thought for a moment, thinking he'd never really lived until he met Evie, and every single day with her had been about taking risks. "There's another problem," he said.

And their eyebrows perked up as they waited for Finch to tell them. "And we're being blamed for it."

***

"Are you going to let her in?" Katie asked.

"I don't know," Evie said. Her face was pinched in deep thought. She looked out the window, watching the little girl holding onto her mother's hand. Her mother doted on her, loved on her, talked sweet to her, like she was the cat's pajamas. The little girl's legs just danced around as if she had ants in her pants.

"Evelyn, please open the door. She has to use the bathroom," Rebecca said, gesturing to the golden-haired little girl.

Katie waited for Evie to do something.

"Eves."

Evie complained under her breath. She wrapped her hand around the door handle and stood there.

"Eeeeeeeves!" Katie screeched.

"Fine!" Evie opened the door and glared at her mother. "She goes pee and then you leave!"

Evie jerked her arm and pointed with her index finger. Her mother whispered to the little girl and gestured for her to go on. The little girl looked up at Evie who pointed in the direction of the bathroom. She hurried down the hall and shut the bathroom door.

"I knew this wasn't going to be easy," Rebecca said. "Hello, Katie," she said, looking at Katie from head to toe and making a face, the kind most people gave Katie when they realized there was a bun in the oven.

"Hi," Katie uttered quietly and fluttered a wave.

"Why are you here?" Evie asked her. "Why?"

"I came to ask you and your father for something," she answered. Evie noticed her skin had a jaundiced look, and wrinkles were etched around the corners of her eyes and thin lips. Her hair was dyed platinum blonde, the kind that you'd get out of a box, and her once flattering figure was gone. Her tight jeans showed the thickness in her thighs and waist. Even her skin had aged: covered in freckles and crinkled like a french fry. The sound of her voice was shrill and scratchy, and her southern accent had faded.

"You're wasting your breath asking me for anything," Evie said.

Her mother took a long, deep breath and rubbed her face. She formed a tight-lipped smile. "You're just like Gray."

"Who are you to talk about Daddy? You left him! You left us!" Evie screamed.

Katie tip-toed out of the room.

"Is he here?" Rebecca asked, searching the room.

"He's dead," Evie said, matter-of-fact. She meant to sound bitter. All of those years of anger were bottled up inside of her and now she was like a volcano erupting. "If you'd been here, you'd know that."

"I'm sorry to hear that," she said quietly.

"I'm sure you really are."

"I deserved that, I guess." She held onto the wall and balanced herself. Even Evie felt a tinge, just a tinge, of sympathy for her. "Just need to rest a second. You mind?" she asked, but she made herself at home anyway. She sat down in the recliner and fanned herself.

The little girl came out of the bathroom and moved toward her mother. "Are you okay, Mommy?" she asked in a pip-squeak voice, stroking her mother's leathery arm.

"Mommy's just tired, Emily," she said. "Just tired."

Evie sat down on the couch, watching them. The little girl played with her shirt and chewed on her pigtails, staring at Evie while their mother labored for breath.

After a moment of resting, Rebecca said to Evie, "This is your sister, Emily." She nudged Emily, and Emily moved hesitantly toward Evie and gave her a light, faint hug, the kind you'd give a sweaty person for fear of touching them.

Evie sat back against the couch cushion and exhaled. "Hi," she said. It wasn't curt, but it wasn't *Pollyanna* either.

"So, will Emily be meeting her daddy, too?" Evie said sharply and cocked a brow at her mother.

CHAPTER 11

"Emily, honey, go outside and play," Rebecca said.

The little girl gave her a hesitant look.

"It's okay." She nudged. "Just give Evelyn and me some time to talk." The way she talked to her really ate at Evie. All nice and gentle, like the picture perfect mother. Evie didn't have any recollection of her mother speaking to her in the same syrupy sweet tone. Her memories were filled with an angry woman who was irritated that Evie was always in the way.

Emily walked to the front door, took one last peek at her mother who gestured for her to go on and stepped outside.

"I guess I should start from the beginning," Rebecca said. She leaned forward, grunting as she shifted in the chair.

"I'll give you five minutes," Evie said. "Then you can go back wherever in the hell it is you came from."

"St. Louis," she said. "You told me to go back from where I came. We live in St. Louis."

She decided to ignore her mother's tongue in cheek comment. She looked for a ring on her hand and didn't see one. "You divorced?"

"From Gray, yes," Rebecca answered. "I wrote you," she added.

"I know. I tore your letter to shreds."

"I called a few times but no one ever answered."

"We carried on with our lives." She let out a heavy sigh and titled her head to the side, pursing her lips. "You married?"

"No," she answered. "Not since Gray."

"Humph," was all that Evie could muster. All that time she'd pictured her mother married to some rich bank executive, living in some fancy house, going out for manicures and playing tennis. She sure as hell didn't think her mother would live in the midwest or be single, and she most definitely didn't think that she'd age as much as she had.

"I've done some horrible things in my life. Dreadful things." She closed her eyes and shook her head.

"And you're here to confess?" Evie snapped. "Because I won't offer my forgiveness."

"I know," Rebecca said. "I don't expect you to."

Evie clicked her shoes against the wooden floor. Her legs bounced up and down.

"Then why are you here?" she asked.

***

Finch and Friedrich decided to drive to the Myers' house to let Mr. Myers know his son was causing trouble, trouble that affected them all. He brought Friedrich along because Friedrich always seemed to be the voice of reason. If ever there was a storm, Friedrich was the calm. He was the one who saw things from a different angle, always showing everyone there was an alternate way to look at things.

"He's not going to be happy hearing about his son," Finch said.

"No one ever likes to hear the truth when it doesn't suit them," Friedrich said.

They pulled onto the Myers' land and got out of the truck, heading to the front door. A few knocks, and Mr. Myers answered it with an unhappy expression.

"Can I help you?" he asked Finch. He refused to make eye contact with Friedrich even though he was standing directly in front of him. It infuriated Finch that he treated Friedrich like he was invisible. That was more of an insult than cursing at him.

"We need to talk to you about Logan," Finch said.

"What about Logan?" he said. He folded his arms across his chest.

Finch stuffed his hands in his pockets and told Mr. Myers he thought Logan was the one who had spray painted their barn and cow, and he was the one going around town stealing, causing problems. It all made sense to Finch now. McDaniels was evil but the graffiti on the barn and the cow, the golf balls, that was something a dumb teenaged kid would do. Finch just didn't see it until he saw Logan tying up that chicken.

Mr. Myers brought his lips up to his nose and scowled. "Ain't my boy. You're mistaken."

"No, sir, I saw him and his friends running away today after they tied up Holt's chicken," Finch said.

Myers jabbed his finger at Finch and said, "I heard you were caught in his hen house trying to steal his chicken and gave it back after Holt aimed his rifle at you."

Finch tried not to laugh but the ridiculousness of it all: stealing chickens. And at his age? Really? As if he would have done it as a teen. He had better things to do when he was Logan's age, like throw knives for a living and make out with girls.

"You think this is funny?" Myers leaned in, flaring his big ole nostrils.

Finch backed away and held up his palms. Friedrich stood between them and said, "We're not laughing at you, but you have to see that it is highly unlikely. We are adults. This is something a child would do as a prank."

"What I see is a tattooed freak standing on my porch with some loser carny who shacks up with a poor young girl who is too busy grievin' over her daddy to see that she's being taken advantage of." He clenched his jaw. "Y'all get off my property, and while you're at it, go back to wherever it is you're from!"

Friedrich sighed quietly, solemnly, and opened his mouth to say something but thought better of it. Finch glared at the man and kept his balled ups fists in his jeans pockets, hoping to God that he could control that temper of his.

"I said," Myers poked his finger in Friedrich's chest, "get off my land!"

Friedrich motioned for Finch to follow him, and they moved to the truck with Myers shouting at them, telling them "To Get!" As if they were racoons sifting through garbage. As Finch sat down in the driver's side, Logan popped from the corner of the house and stared them down, glaring at them. His lips formed a subtle smirk, the kind that told Finch he knew he hadn't been caught.

"It seems that you and Evie may be facing a mountain of obstacles," Friedrich said.

"Yeah," Finch breathed, "and that mountain may be too high to climb."

***

"I was pregnant with Emily when I left," Rebecca started.

Evie's feet and legs quit moving, and she inched closer to the edge of the couch cushion. A part of her wanted to hear the confession. She wanted to know the reasons her mother used to justify leaving them.

"I was a terrible wife to Gray. He was such a good father."

"You weren't so great at mothering either," Evie blurted.

Rebecca took a sharp breath and said, "I never really loved your father."

Evie sat back against the couch, feeling the blow, like she'd just been shot through the heart. All that love her father gave her, and to never have it given back to him? Such a waste, Evie thought.

"I wish I had. He was a good man," she continued.

"He was too good for you."

"Yes, he was," Rebecca agreed. "I never should have married him. He was just an escape, really. And at first, things were fine, but the bliss wore off pretty quick, and I realized I'd made the biggest mistake of my life: marrying a farmer who I didn't love one bit."

"Then why did you stay as long as you did? Why have a kid with him?"

"I wanted a child, and so did Gray," she said. "But that didn't stop me from wanting more, from always thinking the grass was greener."

"You're selfish," Evie spat.

To that, Rebecca didn't respond. "I dated Nate," she said referring to Nate McDaniels, "all through high school and then when I started college. He was everything to me, but he cheated on me, and we broke things off." She looked off as if she was in deep reflection.

"And that's when you met Daddy. I know, he told me," Evie interrupted.

She turned her attention back to Evie. "Yes, that's when I met Gray, and at first things were great. He was everything Nate wasn't: a true gentleman. But when you're young and you think you're in love with an idea, you can't stop obsessing over it," she said and leaned forward, staring Evie deep in the eyes. "I couldn't get Nate out of my system. I thought I loved him; I thought he loved me."

Evie didn't say anything. She had suspected there was more to their relationship when Katie made a few comments; then the memories started flooding in, like the dam had broken. Flashes of her mother's hand lingering longer on Nate's arms when they were at parties. Evie going over to Katie's, and her mother disappearing for hours while she and Katie played dolls. The telephone conversations, hushed and full of twirling hair and big smiles.

"Our affair carried on for most of my marriage to your daddy," she said. "He suspected Nate and I were seeing each other. I didn't hide it; Nate didn't either."

Evie stood up and shouted, "I've heard enough! Just get out, won't you, and don't ever come back!" She hated that tears were welling, but she couldn't stop them from coming.

Rebecca slowly got up from the chair, struggling to catch her breath. "I was pregnant with Emily," she said. "And I told Nate. I thought we'd get married, but when I told him, he was so angry. He blamed me, saying, 'How could you let this happen?' As if I'd done something wrong. I didn't realize it, but he was never going to leave Julia." Rebecca frowned and closed her eyes.

Evie was too startled to move, to do anything. So mad she was seeing red, yet so desperate to hear her out.

"That's when I left. I couldn't expect your father to raise a child that wasn't his, and I just didn't love him, but I didn't want to keep hurting him either."

"He never got over you," Evie said. A lump caught in her throat; it ached for her to talk about her daddy and all that he'd given this woman who never loved him back.

"I moved from town to town, working here and there, never really settling. When Emily was born, I noticed her blue eyes, Gray's eyes, and then her nose: it's small and round like yours, like Gray's was. She has my hair, but she has Gray's face."

"But you said she was Nate's?" Evie placed her hand over her mouth.

"I thought she was. Hell, Nate and I were like rabbits, but Gray and I weren't strangers to the bed either."

Evie glowered at her.

"She's his. She's your full-blooded sister."

"Why didn't you come back?" Evie whispered. "Why?"

"I was already gone, been gone almost a year. I couldn't come crawling back. And he needed to move on without me. Raising Emily with him wasn't going to make me happier," she said. "And…"

Evie knew what was coming but still flinched.

"I didn't love him," Rebecca continued.

"But she was his daughter!"

"I know, and it was wrong for me to keep her from him. He would've loved her," she said with a faint smile. "She's all him."

Evie took a deep breath and wiped at her tears. "What do you want?" she asked. She couldn't stand to hear her mother anymore. She couldn't stand to look at her.

"I came here to ask you and your daddy to take care of Emily for me," Rebecca said. "Life's played a cruel trick on me for all that I've done wrong. I'm dying."

CHAPTER 12

Finch pulled the truck up the drive; a blonde-haired little girl was twirling around on their front lawn and talking to herself. She looked familiar, and then he caught his breath, knowing why. She was the image of Evie.

He noticed the green Ford Falcon parked out front as he walked to the porch. The little girl stopped moving around in a circle and smiled at him.

"Hi," he said and squatted to reach her height. She was small, like Evie.

"Hi," she said.

"What's your name?"

"Emily," she answered. "Who are you?"

"Finch Mills. I'm Evie's fiancé," he said, proudly. Saying fiancé aloud made it real.

"What's a 'fiancé?'" she asked.

"It means we're going to get married," he explained. "How do you know Evie?"

Most people would be surprised to discover that Finch Mills had a way with children. He liked them well enough and talked to them like they were human beings instead of an idiot who didn't know any better. Kids in the carnival liked Finch. They'd cling to him, appreciative he didn't talk down to them.

"Who is Evie?"

"Evelyn, I mean," he corrected. Evie had told him that her mother always called her by her given name, and it drove her crazy. Finch made a mental note to never call her Evelyn, even when he was angry with her.

"She's my sister," Emily said, matter-of-fact.

He nodded and then stood up. He offered her his hand and said, "Want some Coca Cola?"

She nodded and smiled. "Yeah, it's boring out here, but Mommy said I had to play while she and Evelyn talked."

He offered her his hand, and they walked around the side of the house to the kitchen. This was turning into a shit storm of a day, he thought.

***

Evie didn't know what to say or how to respond. Dying? She felt nothing. Absolutely nothing. Not a speck of remorse or sorrow at the news. She'd built a fortress around her heart when it came to her mother, and nothing would make that stone wall crumble. Not even the woman's mortality.

She wasn't going to say sorry. She wasn't going to pat her on the hand and offer her a sympathetic, "there, there." She wasn't going to spill any tears. What'd she care? She'd been dead to her for years. She didn't feel a lick of sadness. She had felt more when one of her newborn calves died.

Rebecca didn't seem surprised that Evie wasn't startled or shaken up by the news. "I've got ovarian cancer. The doctors say there isn't anything that can be done."

"How long?" Evie said, her voice was even, monotone, like she was asking what the weather was going to be like tomorrow or what dressing she wanted on her salad.

"A few months," she said. "Maybe more. Maybe less."

"And you wanted us to raise Emily?"

Rebecca nodded slowly. "I didn't know your daddy…"

"Well, he is, and now you've got yourself in a pickle, don't you?"

"I don't have anyone else. My parents are gone, and I don't have any brothers or sisters," she said. "Y'all were it, and if you don't agree to help, she'll be all alone. She doesn't deserve that. No matter how much hatred you have for me, you can't take it out on her."

Before Evie could respond, Finch and Emily came into the living room. Chocolate ice cream covered her mouth.

"Mommy!" She rushed toward Rebecca and wrapped her arms around her. "Finch gave me Coke and chocolate ice cream."

Rebecca faked a laugh. "And who is Finch?" she narrowed her eyes to Evie's.

"He's her fancy," Emily said.

Rebecca laughed. "You mean, fiancé," she corrected. "So, you're getting married?" she asked Evie.

Evie didn't respond. She wasn't planning to share any details about her life with her.

Finch didn't know what to do. He couldn't shake the woman's hand or introduce himself, not the way Evie had talked about her, the way she tore Evie up so much.

"Well, it looks like you've got good taste," Rebecca added, scanning Finch up and down. "Y'all will make pretty babies."

She didn't need her mother's approval, and she didn't like the way her mother was looking at Finch like he was chocolate on a stick. "I think it's time you got going," Evie snapped. Enough was enough. The woman crawled under her skin.

"I hear you," Rebecca said and grabbed onto Emily's hand. "Just think about what we talked about. It's all on you, now, Evelyn," she added. "Say bye to your sister, Emily."

Emily gave Evie a faint hug and then hugged Finch even tighter and smiled up at him.

"We're planning to eat dinner at The Diner tonight around seven o'clock. Maybe you can join us," Rebecca said before clicking on her heels and leaving.

Katie rushed down the stairs the moment the door closed. "I heard everything." Her face was red, and Evie assumed she'd been crying because her hazel eyes were bloodshot and she was sniffling.

"I figured," Evie said with a frown.

"I never knew," she said. "All this time he was cheating on my mom."

"I'm sorry," Evie said, but sorry for what? That her mother and Katie's father were cheaters. That they should have ended up together because they seemed to be cut from the same cloth: the same dirty cloth. "I put two and two together," Evie said. "Then she confirmed what I'd already suspected."

"To think that Emily could've been my sister," Katie said.

"To think that you and I could've been sisters," Evie said. The thought had crossed her mind, and it wasn't a stretch, but thank God for miracles because she knew with all her heart and good DNA she was a Barnes.

She pulled on her braid and twisted her lips. She glanced at Finch and said, "We've got ourselves a quandary."

***

Finch and Evie held hands as they trekked through the grass. The sun was setting, creating a myriad of colors: orange, purple, and blue, shades so serene you'd think they would have stopped to kiss and hold each other, celebrating their love. But reality was staring them in their faces, and love had to take a backseat.

"A sister?" he said. "I knew the moment I saw her."

"She looks just like me, doesn't she?"

"Yeah," he said and raked his fingers through his hair. "All of this is happening at once."

"That's usually the way it works, isn't it?"

"First my job, then that damn Myers kid, and now this." He hopped up on the fence and extended his hand to hers. She joined him and together they sat staring at the sky, at the horizon in front of them. Silence pervaded, and both of them were too deep in thought to say anything.

"What are you going to do?" he asked her.

She turned to face him. "If your father showed up in the same situation what would you do?"

"This isn't about me."

"That's a cop out, Finch. Just answer the question."

"Well." He scratched at his scalp, "I'd do what I thought was right."

"For who? Right for who?"

"For the kid," he answered. "I'd do what was right for the kid."

"I feel bad, being so mean to *her*," Evie confessed. She still referred to Rebecca as a pronoun.

"You have your right. I wasn't so kind to David last time I saw him." He thought about their conversation, how he'd told him he'd never see him again, but he was okay with that. He was fine with shutting him out of his life forever.

"She doesn't seem too sorry for what she did to me and Daddy," Evie said with sadness. "She just wants someone to take care of Emily."

"You've got to make your decision based on what you think you're capable of."

"I don't know if I can raise a kid."

"You can do anything you want to, Evie. You're stronger than an ox," he said with a proud smile.

"What about us? We'd be starting our marriage off with a kid," she said with a frown.

"We're already starting off with a million obstacles, might as well add another," he said and then thought for a moment. "But this is your choice. I'm not telling you what to do. You have to do what you think is right."

"Guess we're eating dinner at The Diner tonight, aren't we?" She jumped off of the fence. "Want to sleep under the stars tonight?"

"What?" he made a face. "You are so random."

She tugged on his hand. He got off of the fence and stood in front of her with their hands linked together.

"Everything's about to change," she said.

"Change how?"

"I'm not going to desert her, so it seems we're going to have another mouth to feed," she said. "I just can't do it to her, Finch. I don't care how much I hate Rebecca, Emily's my family. She's a part of Daddy, and I just can't leave her to the wolves."

He leaned down to kiss her on the corner of her mouth. "I love you."

"Good, because we're going to need all the love we have to deal with everything that's coming our way."

***

Rebecca and Emily sat in a booth sharing a milkshake. Both of them slurped on their straws and giggled like they were laughing at some inside joke. Finch read the pain all over Evie's face. The hurt she felt. The envy, jealousy, whatever you wanted to call it, that filled her. He couldn't blame her. He'd feel the same if he saw David playing catch or fishing with another kid, doing all of the things he should have done with him.

All the tales she had told him about growing up, about Rebecca always chastising her, getting on to her for this or that, never fully satisfied with her, and there she sat with her other daughter treating her like she walked on water. Maybe some of it had to do with the fact that she was dying. People had a change of heart when death's door was open to them. They got nicer, fearful of the unknown, of what was to come. Most people worried about the afterlife, where they'd end up, and in Rebecca's case, maybe she sinned so much she was trying to make up for it. Whatever the case, Evie's hand tightened into Finch's, and her face was pinched and red.

Emily looked so much like Evie, and she even did this thing that Evie did, sighing with a crinkle in her nose when she didn't like something. He'd witnessed it when they had ice cream together. It made him feel an instant connection to the girl, like he was meeting Evie when she was nine years of age.

They sat across from Emily and Rebecca. Their giggling had stopped. Rebecca's face was hard to read: surprised, pleased, hurt. He couldn't tell. He was good about people. All his years on the circuit made him an expert at reading them. If they were liars, cheats, soulless, he could tell. With her, it was all business with Evie. There was a wall there, a big fortress, and something a little more. It was almost as if the woman resented Evie. But what could she hate Evie for? Maybe because Evie was everything she wasn't. Finch felt David's jealousy of him. It was a strange feeling, having a parent in competition with their own kid, but people like David and Rebecca never grew up; they only got older. Finch turned his attention to

Emily, who just smiled wide at him like he was Santa Claus on Christmas day.

"Hi," she said. Chocolate covered her lips.

"Hey," he shot back with a grin. He was tempted to pinch her nose.

"So you came," Rebecca said in a tired voice. Black shadows crept under her dark eyes, and the fluorescent lighting highlighted the few springy white hairs peeping up on top of her head.

"So we did," Evie said. The sarcasm was evident in her tone. Finch felt the hatred permeating the air.

"You used to love coming here," Rebecca started.

Evie made a face and held on tightly to Finch's hand. He flinched. Sometimes those little hands and feet of hers took him by surprise. She was tougher than she looked.

"We'd order a burger and fries and share a milkshake just like me and Emily just did." She smiled at Emily as she said it. "And then we'd argue over who got the cherry. Do you remember that?" Rebecca said to Evie.

"I remember lots of things," Evie said. Everyone but Emily knew what that undertone of that statement was.

"So, you were in the carnival?" Rebecca asked Finch.

"Yes." He figured it was safer to answer her with short answers and not give away too much detail. They weren't going to chat it up like she was trying so hard to do.

"That must have been interesting," she said. "I only went that one time..."

"Before you left," Evie spoke up. "It was before you left." She glared at Rebecca and gestured to the waitress. "I'll have a Coke float."

"Just a Coke," Finch said.

The waitress walked away. "I don't care for milkshakes anymore. I haven't in a long time," Evie said.

Even Finch saw the childish nature behind Evie's choice of words. She was searching to hurt Rebecca any way that she could. He couldn't fault her. The woman abandoned her, and Evie never got a chance to say her piece. Now she had it, and she was taking every opportunity she had to punch the woman right where it hurt.

"People's tastes change," Rebecca said.

"With some it's more frequent," she said.

"When are you getting married?" Rebecca asked.

"Soon," Evie said. "It's going to be a small wedding. Only close friends are invited."

"Am I invited?" Emily asked.

"Of course," Finch chimed in. "You can be the flower girl."

She offered him a smile and sucked on her straw, finishing off the rest of the thick milkshake.

The waitress brought the Coke float and Coke to the table, sliding them toward Finch and Evie. Evie stirred the contents of vanilla ice cream and Coca Cola, turning the liquid into a light brown color. She sipped and sat back against the vinyl cushioned seating.

Finch inhaled his drink, thinking that there were plenty of other places he'd rather be than sitting right there in the thick of it. The tension was high, and even if Emily was a little girl, she had to know there was a big band of hate between Evie and her mother.

Rebecca reached into her purse and pulled out a dime. She handed it to Emily and said, "Here. Go choose a song on that juke box." She pointed to the colorful source of music in the corner of the restaurant.

Emily leapt at the chance and ran over to the juke box.

"Are you going to take her?" Rebecca asked in a hushed voice.

Evie nodded.

She breathed a sigh of relief and sat back in a more relaxed position. "She's allergic to strawberries, and she's a hard worker and loves animals." She listed with her hands. "She'll work real hard for you on the farm. She's real smart but struggles in school some. Just be patient with her and help her with her homework. And don't let her eat sweets late at night because she'll be up forever." She took in a deep breath and thought for a moment. "She has a sweetness in her that you and I don't..."

Finch saw that Evie took offense to that. Hell, he took it personally. Saying Evie wasn't sweet was a bold faced lie. Evie was all things good. She was like all things beautiful. That was one of the things he loved most about her – her ability to see beyond the first layer, that she loved unconditionally.

"Evie is one of the truest people I've ever met," he defended.

"She was a fussy child. Always fighting with me for this or that. Never seemed to be satisfied," Rebecca said.

"Children have strong radars..." he started, feeling the anger building. Evie touched his thigh and shot him a look, one that told him it wasn't worth it.

"Young love is the best. The newness and lack of judgment. You don't see the flaws. That'll change soon enough," she said with a frown. "No matter how much you think you're in love."

Before either Finch or Evie could respond, Emily came running back to the booth. "I picked a song!" she sang.

"Good, honey," Rebecca said.

"You hear it?" Emily said.

"Yes. It's one of my favorites," Rebecca said. Sam Cooke's "You Send Me" played.

"I'm surprised it isn't 'Your Cheatin' Heart,'" Evie said.

"I'm not much of a Hank Williams fan," Rebecca said.

"Too close to home for you?" Evie said.

"Why don't you take care of the bill?" Rebecca said to Emily. She handed her a crisp five dollar bill. Emily got up and walked to the cash register. "You hate me, I get it. But no matter what, you have to promise me that you won't taint her image of me when I'm gone. She loves me, and I don't want you spoiling that."

"If you're worried that I'm going to tell her that you cheated on Daddy, that you left without a hint of remorse, that you kept her from her own Daddy because you thought she was someone else's daughter, well, don't worry," Evie snapped. "She can form her own opinion as she gets older. But, if she asks me questions, I'll tell her the truth. I won't sugar coat it. I'll tell her what she wants to know. Just 'cause you're dead doesn't make you a saint."

Rebecca sat back, like the wind had been kicked out of her. "I guess I have no choice then, do I?"

"No, you don't," Evie said, folding her arms against her chest. "You sure don't."

"I'll be dead and won't be able to defend whatever it is you say."

"Like I said, I will only tell her the truth if she asks about you," Evie said. "I won't make snide comments or tell her how I really feel about you."

"Just promise to take care of her." Rebecca reached across the table and touched Evie's arm. She flinched from the contact and brought her folded arms closer to her chest. "I'll be by tomorrow in the morning."

"You're not going to go back to St. Louis first?" Evie asked.

"No. The drive is too much to go back and forth."

Finch noticed Rebecca's eyes shifted as she said it but he wasn't going to make mention of it to Evie.

"Well, we'll see you tomorrow, then," Evie said and quieted once Emily came running back to the booth.

***

Later that night Evie and Finch lay under the stars. The sky was cloudless, giving them a clear view of Orion. Evie nestled to Finch and rested her head on his shoulders. He wrapped the blanket tight around them and held her as close as he could.

"It's times like this that make me think there isn't much beauty in the world," she said quietly. The entire incident with her mom had unsettled her. All that time she wanted to tell her mother off, make her feel all the hurt and pain she'd felt all of those years, but now that she was back, Evie saw that being hateful to her only made her feel worse. It didn't take away the truth: she had left her. Hating her took so much energy, just like Gray had told her, and now as she lay there exhausted, she knew why he said that. Hate took effort, apathy didn't. She was going to let it all go; otherwise, she'd spend the rest of her life chewed up inside for something that could never be changed.

"As long as you're in it, there is," he murmured.

Sometimes the man surprised her. He rarely offered compliments or mushy words of love, but sometimes he'd say the kindest, most thoughtful thing. Evie would just want to hold him and tell him how much she loved him. "Why Finch Mills, I think you've become a hopeless romantic." She turned to face him and smiled.

"Not hopeless, just crazy in love is all," he said and kissed her.

CHAPTER 13

It was eleven o'clock in the morning, and Rebecca still hadn't shown up. Evie got a bad feeling in her gut. Tired of watching the clock and waiting for Rebecca to show up, she and Finch decided instead to go to the motel where she was staying.

Evie couldn't believe that in a matter of hours she was going to be raising a kid. She'd called Spence, Cooper's and Preston's brother who was an attorney, and he had told her there would be paper work to fill out, but since Rebecca was dying the state wouldn't petition.

"They like for family to stay together," he had said.

She had made the decision quickly. Blood was blood, and Emily was her sister. She couldn't leave her even if she hated her mother, even if her mother didn't deserve her help. That didn't matter. All that mattered was Emily and making sure she was okay.

Finch supported her. "I'd do the same," he told her. "If David had a brood of kids, I couldn't leave them, no matter what."

"We'll have to wait on applying for our marriage certificate."

For a split second, before Rebecca had shown up, he thought about giving up, leaving Evie so that she could marry a man people wouldn't despise, so she could live her life happily and quietly without any drama. But then his senses came back: he knew that leaving her would not only break his heart, but it'd also break hers. He was going to have to deal with everything that was being thrown at them. The good and the bad. The ugly and the pretty. The stuff that people wanted to shove in a closet and forget about but they just couldn't because it had to be dealt with. The sweet stuff that people shouted at the moon for. All of it. It came as one package.

"I figured," he said.

"It's not what I want," she told him. "To wait, I mean."

"Me neither, but life is telling us differently."

Shady Rest Motel was out on the far side of town. Truckers stayed there. People having affairs did, too. Evie wondered if this was where Rebecca and Nate met. Or were they so blatant that they shacked up on her daddy's land? The thought gave her the shivers and made her despise Nate more than before. Every time he was around Gray, he had a smug look on his face, and now Evie knew what it meant. He was like some alpha dog raising his leg up and pissing on everything, just as Finch had described him.

The only other types to stay at Shady Rest Motel were those passing through town, stopping for a night before getting back on the interstate. It wasn't a motel where kids played in the pool. It wasn't the type of place people called to make reservations. It was a quick, split-decision type of establishment. One where a wary driver pulled off the road and lay his head at night for a decent night's sleep. One where a family was trying to skimp by and figured they could afford a night there.

Evie had never stepped foot on the property, just passed it by a few times here and there. Her daddy told her to stay away from the place. "Only trash goes there," he said one time. And maybe he had known. Maybe Rebecca and Nate carried on there, met like two thieves in the night expressing their burning desires for each other without a care for anyone else. Maybe that whole time, Gray knew and just decided to ignore it because he suffered from stupid love. The kind of love that made any reasonable person an idiot.

Shady Rest Motel needed a paint job, and the pool was drained of water. A little boy sat on the pool deck. His legs dangled over the edge. He kicked the concrete as he blew bubbles. The parking lot was sparse, with the exception of a station wagon and a beat-up Pinto.

They approached the motel clerk, who banged on the television and adjusted its antennas. Evie saw a glimpse of his hairy stomach through his tight button-down top. A few buttons had popped off, and his belly collapsed over his dirty britches.

"Damn TV!" he shouted and glanced their way, gazing at Evie. He licked his lips and narrowed his eyes to her chest.

"We're looking for Rebecca Barnes," Finch said, moving in front of her. He smelled lust all over the wretched man.

The clerk glanced down before taking another lingering look at Evie. Only a few names were entered in the register.

"Can you tell us what room she's staying in?" Finch asked.

"It will cost you," he said. "Ain't s'posed to just give out names."

Finch tapped on his knife and said, "I didn't carry any money with me." His expression was serious, and he kept his hands on his knife handle.

The man cleared his throat and said, "Twelve. She's in room twelve."

Finch grabbed Evie by the hand, and they headed out of that dingy office that wreaked of pot and cheap booze.

"Were you going to knife him?" Evie asked, her voice shaky and unsteady.

"Evie." He laughed. "No. You're always thinking I'm just waiting to put a horse's head in someone's bed."

"Well, you sure scared me."

He stopped and placed his palm gently against her cheek. "I needed to intimidate him, and I didn't like the way he was staring at you." He didn't like it at all. Matter-of-fact, he was tempted to punch the guy in the gut for staring at Evie like she was a piece of candy.

"I can handle a dirty old man staring at me," she said. "What if he had a gun? He could've pulled it out and threatened you with it."

"He could have, but he didn't. We've got the room number, don't we?" he said, stepping forward. Evie stopped and folded her arms against her chest.

"What?" Finch asked with frustration.

"You've got to be careful. If something happened to you..."

"What, Evie?" he asked, inching closer and wrapping his arms around her waist.

"Oh nothing," she moaned in frustration.

He laughed and drew her closer, touching her hair and kissing at her neck and cheeks. Forget the kid, he thought, he could stay there all day kissing her like that.

She pulled away and waved her finger at him. "We came here for a reason."

He sighed and followed her to Rebecca's room. Evie knocked a few times and didn't get an answer. "Think she's gone?" she asked.

He shrugged and said, "I don't know."

Evie knocked harder on the door.

Finch tapped Evie on the arm and said, "Look." He pointed to the front window, at the fingers holding onto the heavy drapes and the set of blue eyes staring at them.

"Emily," Evie said. "Will you let us in?"

The door knob slowly moved to the left, and Emily opened the door. Her face was red and puffy; tears trickled down her chubby cheeks. She was in her pajamas, and the television was on.

The room smelled old and dusty. Like a room that'd been shit on and forgotten about. And the décor wasn't much better: green shaggy carpet, brown curtains with dust covering the hems and paint peeling off of the concrete walls. A coin machine sat next to the bed. For twenty-five cents you could have the bed vibrate. The headboard was nailed to the wall, and the orange bedspread had cigarette burns engrained in the chenille threading.

Evie scrunched her face, bringing her hand up to her nose. "Where's your mother?"

"I don't know," she answered with a sniffle. "I woke up, and she was gone."

Evie gave Finch a look, and he just shook his head.

"I'm sure she'll come back real soon," Evie lied. She smelled a big rat, the kind that festered and left a trail of turds.

"How long have you been awake?" Evie asked.

Emily shrugged. "I don't know."

She sighed and sat on the edge of the bed. Finch joined her, and together they all three sat watching the television: Emily enthralled by the small screen, and Finch and Evie wondering when they should leave. When did the clock give them permission to go?

Hours had passed. "I'm hungry," Emily complained.

"We should get some lunch," Finch said.

Evie agreed. "We'll come back here after you've eaten."

But Finch told Emily to pack her stuff, that her mother would know where to find them because he was going to leave a note for her, and Evie gave him a questioning look. He kept writing the note and uttered quietly to her, "She's not coming back, Evie."

Evie didn't dispute that. She knew Rebecca Barnes well enough. At least she hadn't dropped Emily off like those sorry bastards who tired of their yappy dogs and left them out in the middle of nowhere to fend for themselves. At least she had the decency to make sure she was in the same town as Evie, but to leave her in a motel room? The woman was evil, living evil, and she shivered as she realized what a loathsome creature her mother really was. Knowing that a man as good as her daddy loved her, cared for her, thought she'd hung the moon, and the whole time she was just passing by, waiting for the next big thing. Well, her next big thing was death, and Evie wasn't sad she was dying. She felt for Emily because she knew what it was to lose her mother, but she was numb for her own feelings. Discovering that your own flesh and blood is everything you detest in someone, that they are a heartless soul who'd abandon a nine-year-old little girl, made her feel sick. Sick to her stomach. Sick in her head. Sick in her soul.

Finch picked Emily up and carried her to the truck. She laughed and laughed, begging him to helicopter spin her some more. They'd been together for less than a day and had already established a bond. But Finch was magnetic that way. Animals loved him. Why wouldn't kids?

Evie drove toward her house and watched as her little sister's legs kicked back and forth against the truck seat. She fiddled with her thumbs and chewed on her hair. She was a basket of nerves, and all Evie could do was pat her gently on the knee.

Finch cocked a brow, noticing Evie's gesture, and brought his gaze back out the window. It was overcast and gray, and the weather wasn't cooperating. And it was a cold day. Bitter cold. Too frigid for fall.

He was silent. Evie wondered if he'd decided to fly the nest because of every terrible thing coming at them. She wouldn't blame him if he did.

They walked inside of the house. Katie was cleaning again. She set the can of dust polish and a rag down on the table and wiped her hands. "Hi," she said to them all.

"Katie, this is Emily," Evie said.

Emily reached out to hug Katie and then said, "You're having a baby."

Katie laughed. "That's right. How'd you guess?"

But Emily didn't get the sarcasm. "Your stomach," she answered with a strange face.

"Her mom went out for a while, so we'd figure we'd come here and eat," Evie said and mouthed to Katie, "She left."

Katie nodded, giving Evie a sad look and wrapped her arm around Emily. "How about a sandwich?"

Emily shook her head and smiled.

"We'll catch up to y'all in just a minute," Evie hollered as Katie and Emily marched back to the kitchen. She pushed the front door open and stood out on the porch. The wind swept by her. She wrapped her arms around her chest.

Finch warmed her with his hands.

"She up and left," Evie said.

"Maybe she went somewhere and is coming back?" he offered, but even he knew that was a hopeless prospect.

"She's a deserter, Finch. Once she knew we were going to take care of Emily, she made up her mind to pawn her off like a piece of a China dish." She faced the cold brittle wind and trembled. Finch rubbed her arms and kissed her on the forehead, which didn't offer the solace Evie was seeking.

"If you want out, now is the time," she said.

He stepped back and made a face, one that was hurt and startled.

"I don't want you to."

"Then quit being a martyr," he said. "Don't say stuff like that. It's just..."

"Stupid," she answered for him.

"Evie, I'm in this forever. With the good and the bad."

A part of her felt relieved: hearing him say it to her was enough consolation. Like even though this craziness was happening, he was holding her hand through the winds and the storms and all of the fury that life threw at them.

"How are we going to handle this situation?" she asked him and leaned her head against his chest.

"We just will, Evie," he said and kissed the top of her head. "We just will." But even he wondered how they were going to get through it all.

***

The hands on the clock moved round and round, and Rebecca never showed up. Emily would peer out the window or suddenly get up from where she was sitting, thinking it was a knock on the door or the sound of footsteps on their porch, when it was just the house settling or the wind howling. A look of disappointment would wash over her face each and every time. And the more that it happened, the more Evie felt that ache. That terrible, terrible ache.

"When is Mommy coming?" she'd ask them. Finch and Katie tried to occupy her, playing a game of checkers and watching shows only a kid would like, and it'd work for a while, but then she'd scan the room, stare at the door and ask again.

Evie decided to let Emily sleep in her room. She begged Evie to tuck her in. Evie didn't know what being "tucked in" meant. Gray had always shouted downstairs for her to brush her teeth and get to sleep, and that was that. But Emily wanted Evie, Finch and Katie to walk her upstairs, fix her blankets all snug, and keep the light on for her.

"For the love of Pete," Evie said. "Can't we just send her to bed?" She was already seeing the challenges of having a kid around, and she felt completely and utterly useless when it came to children.

Katie shot her a look. "She's scared, Eves."

This made Evie feel even more inept in the child rearing department.

Finch told Emily some tale about the carnival that piqued Katie and Evie's interests, as well. They were all ears as Finch relayed a story about Rex, who touted himself "The World's Tallest Man" and his love for Dorothy, "The World's Smallest Woman." Emily was enthralled, hanging onto every word he uttered, like he was puffing out magic.

He pulled the covers over her and patted her on the head. Evie just stood there watching him with her mouth open, amazed, then a little jealous that she lacked any skills in that area. Emily clung to Finch and Katie, and there was Evie off to the side like a third wheel.

Katie turned on the side table lamp and said, "We'll leave the door open for you."

"And we're just downstairs," Finch added.

"You're sure to hear a bunch of noises up here. It's just the house so no need to get scared," Evie said. Finch and Katie shot her a look, the kind that said, soften up. "But if you do, we're not far," she added, and Finch and Katie nodded in approval.

Emily closed her eyes and started to nod off. Evie took one last look at her little sister before she left the room.

***

She opened the door to Gray's room. It had been a while since she'd gone in there. Everything was still left in its place. Nothing had been touched or moved: his clothes still hung in the closet, a bottle of cheap aftershave was on his dresser alongside a picture of Evie, and his favorite pair of boots was lined up near the door. Katie had gone in there a few times to dust the furniture and sweep the floor, but that was the extent of it. Evie said she wasn't ready to part with his stuff yet. She wasn't ready to change anything. It had stayed frozen in time like a display at a museum.

"I guess we'll have to sleep in Daddy's room. Emily can sleep in mine," she had said to Finch earlier that night.

He instantly shook his head. "I'll sleep on the couch."

"Why?"

"Evie," he said with a deep breath. " I'm not sleeping with you in your dad's room until we're married."

"You sleep in my room with me."

"That's different."

She didn't argue. Finch had his rules, his ideals and things that he thought were important in their relationship. Things that he thought mattered and were right.

She entered the room and lay down on the bed, still smelling her daddy, or at least telling herself she did. It'd been several months since he died, and she knew there was no way that his scent still lingered, but she swore she smelled him when she lay her head on his pillow.

She sobbed quietly, wondering how in the world she was going to raise a little girl whose mother just up and left. Rebecca Barnes had done it again: walked away and left without any remorse. Evie closed her damp eyes, wondering what the next day and days after had in store for her and Finch.

Finch lightly tapped on the door and said in a hushed tone, "Evie. You okay?" She sniffled, and he came over to her and kneeled beside her. "You're crying," he said.

"I just miss Daddy, and now I've got to raise a sister I don't even know. And you, you lost your job. Everyone in this town is stupid," she rambled, letting it all out without taking a breath. And Finch stayed there, stroking her arm and raking his fingers through her long blonde hair. He pulled her to him and hugged her, telling her that it was going to be okay. That everything was going to be okay.

***

Finch had found it: a stuffed envelope laying on the front porch. Tripod was sniffing it as Finch opened the front door to feed him some bacon. He bent down and picked it up. It wasn't light, and the handwriting on front was pretty, like calligraphy, like a woman's. It was addressed to Evie. He knew who it was from.

He handed Tripod his bacon. Tripod hobbled over to his nesting place on the corner of the porch. Finch stood up and carried the envelope with him in the house. It wasn't his to open, but he was curious as a cat and hoped Evie would rip it open as soon as he gave it to her.

He handed it to her, and she made that face, the one that told him she was annoyed.

"It's from *her*," she said, enunciating the "her." She was always a pronoun. A nameless pronoun. That's how she was known around that house.

"What's in it?"

She half-shrugged and pushed it to the side.

"Evie."

"Fine," she huffed and ripped it open. A folded piece of paper addressed with her name on it and stacks of dollar bills were inside.

She set the card aside and looked at the bills with wide eyes. "Finch, it's a lot of cash."

He picked up the bills and fanned them, gauging how much was bound together in the stack. "There's a lot here, Evie," he said. "A lot."

She picked up the letter and unfolded it. Finch watched as she bit her lip. He cringed at the sight of her teeth clenched hard on her bottom plump lip.

"Dear Evelyn,

I know this is not enough to cover all of the costs for raising a child but I hope that it will help some. I couldn't handle saying goodbye to Emily. It's better this way. It's better for her, better for me.

I can see that time does not heal all wounds and that you'll never forgive me for walking out on you and your father. You were better off being raised by him and maybe, in time, you'll see that. You and I may be mother and daughter, but we're as different as night and day. And you would've ended up resenting me anyway.

Please take care of my little girl. She's precious and so needy. She needs to know you love her. Love her like you couldn't love me.

Rebecca

Evie let out a deep breath, she'd been holding in air while she read the letter. Finch saw her veins showing, and her face was blemished.

"Here," she said, sliding it in his direction. "She's never going to apologize."

Finch read the letter and then folded it into a neat perfect square. He gave it back to Evie, who tossed it in the garbage without a moment's hesitation.

"It's a load of shit, you know."

What could he say? That he agreed with her. That her mother was selfish, and here was her chance to make amends and all she could do was lay the blame on Evie because they were different. Because her mother was immature and a coward.

"That it is," he agreed quietly.

She wiped her eyes with her arm and shot up. "Well, I don't have time for a pity party. I've got some cows to feed." She stepped into her rubber boots and shoved the kitchen door open, without waiting for a response from Finch.

She was half-way to the barn before she remembered Emily was there. She turned on her heels and stomped to the door, mumbling like a crazy woman on her way there.

Finch smiled, the kind that told her he'd known before she even realized it.

"Do I have to wake her up?" Evie asked him.

Finch shrugged. "Probably."

"And I have to feed her, too?" Evie pressed.

"She's not a cow, but yes, Evie, she has to eat," he teased.

She shot him a dirty look, then softened, almost growing panicky as her blue eyes darted back and forth. "Good Lord, Finch, I don't know a thing about kids."

He patted her on the shoulder, trying not to seem like he was patronizing her. "You'll figure it out."

"And when are we going to tell her?"

He grew serious. "The sooner the better, Evie."

Evie, with Friedrich, Mouse and Finch's help, fed the cows. It didn't take that long with the four of them, and Evie even thought Friedrich and Mouse were worth their weight. "They've caught on," she said to Finch. Doris, on the other hand, wasn't cut out for that kind of work, and she had hinted at working as a nurse again.

"I was an LPN before I worked in the carnival," she had said one night at dinner. "Just would have to take a few refresher courses is all, and I could be of some use."

And Evie encouraged Doris because she wasn't an indentured servant. If anything, Evie owed them, all of them: Finch, Mouse, Doris, and Friedrich. She owed them for saving her father's land, and they didn't need to work to prove anything to her. Family was family, and that's what they'd become.

Finch, she figured, was better at fixing things, like things that needed to be repaired around the house. He'd even fixed the loose steps on the front porch, the weathered fences, and the deteriorating chicken coop, which had started to crumble years ago but Gray never had the time. Time— they never seemed to have enough of it when it was just the two of them.

Finch was born to fix things. She was going to take it upon herself to speak to the uppity stupid heads who were responsible for him getting fired so she could change their minds. Certainly after they heard her plea, they'd see reason. She had hope they would anyway. Finch was not born to work as a cow farmer. This she knew within the first few weeks. But he tried and he cared. Oh, how he cared so much about her daddy's land. And that passion was one of the things she loved most about him.

Finch said he'd hold her hand while she broke the news to Emily, and Katie said she'd sit right next to her and do the same. They weren't leaving her to do this unwanted task on her own. But this was Evie's job, and she couldn't rely on either one of them. What she had to tell had to be from her only.

She wiped the sweat off of her forehead and took a long hard swallow of a big ice cold glass of water. What was coming next wasn't going to be easy, and truth be told, she'd been putting it off all day, hoping it'd go away. But then, she took a look at her little sister and after seeing the sadness in those blue eyes of hers, it was like Evie read her mind. Emily knew. Even a nine-year-old knows when their mother has up and left. Even a nine-year-old can be perceptive about people and know when they're lower than the roly poly's who fed off her cows' manure.

She asked Emily to join her outside for a stroll around the property. She got a queasy feeling doing it that way: it made her feel like a character from *The Godfather* taking some poor old soul out to the middle of nowhere to off him. Only she was going to tell Emily that her mother was gone. She'd leave out all of the parts about her mother that she didn't need to know: that Rebecca was selfish and heartless, that she was a philanderer and didn't love their father, and that she was too scared to say goodbye.

And Evie told her, in the most gentle way she could muster, and held onto her little sister, hugging her as she sobbed. Then chased after her when she ran away to cry some more. Evie wasn't going to leave her alone, and she told her that. From there on out they were a team.

She tried to think of all of the things that she wished Gray would've said, and then she said some of the things he did say to her when her mother left. Things like, "You'll never be alone because you've got love right here." And she tightened her hand into a fist and pressed it against her rapidly beating heart. "Even if we're strangers, we're linked by love. A sister's love never flickers out," she said. She uttered words and phrases that she'd never even thought to say until that moment, and at that time, Evie thought she could do this. She could raise that little girl and love her the way she wished her mother had loved her. "I'll never give up on you. Ever."

The sun was setting and the two joined hands, making their way to the house. They stopped for a moment, and Evie said, "Look at that sunset."

Emily nodded slowly and wiped the tears away from her eyes.

"See that?" Evie pointed.

Emily muttered a faint "Yes."

"The sun comes back, Emily. Every day. It may go away, but it always rises the next morning," she said and pointed her thumb to her chest. "That's me. I'll always be here for you just like the sun."

CHAPTER 14

Tripod paced the porch, howling while he hobbled from one side to the other. Evie tried to quiet him, but he wouldn't budge. A little tap on his head didn't stop him from letting out a yelp or shrill cry. "What's the matter, boy?" She searched his eyes and patted him gently. He hovered close for a moment, then scurried to the far end of the porch.

She scratched at her head and pinched her face. Must be old age, she thought. She'd heard about dogs losing their marbles the older they got, doing strange things like this. She shrugged her shoulders and hoped this wasn't going to be the norm for the old dog. She'd had him since she was a toddler. Truthfully, he was Gray's dog. He'd follow Gray to the moon and back, and Gray was known to lift him up and put him in his lap while he rode the ATV and shouted at the cattle.

She frowned, thinking that everything that reminded her of her daddy was either gone or aging. And Tripod was just more proof that life wasn't going to stand still for her, no matter how much she wanted it to.

Sweat trickled down the back of her neck. She took off her jacket and draped it over her shoulder. Even though a colorful array of leaves was starting to fill the trees, the air was sweltering hot, like the middle of summer, and definitely not like an autumn day.

She headed to her truck and left Friedrich, Mouse and Finch to take care of the cows. Doris was nowhere to be found. Friedrich hinted that she had the blues. "She's very morose," he had whispered to them one morning. "She feels useless." Evie asked him why she didn't go back into nursing, and he just shook his head with a frown. "She's afraid no one will hire her around here. I keep telling her to do it. She would be a great nurse, wouldn't she?" He said it with pride. His wide smile was full of life and love. Evie figured that out of everyone she knew, Doris and Friedrich had a deep, special love— the kind you read about in books or watched in the movies. They didn't let their differences affect their relationship. It seemed to strengthen it, and Evie hoped that one day she and Finch would be just like them.

Hearing Friedrich tell her that he thought Doris wouldn't be hired because of who she was and knowing that Finch was being blamed for things he hadn't done incited Evie to take a trip downtown and give some people a piece of her mind. She suspected who the culprits were but wanted to double-check with Mike. No sense in getting irate with the wrong people, she thought. That would only make matters worse, and as far as things were going for her in that small town, she was low on the totem pole if not at the bottom of it.

The volume to Mike's radio was set high, and his scruffy black tennis shoes stuck out from underneath the brown Oldsmobile Cutlass. Evie shouted and nudged his shoes with her foot. He rolled from underneath the car, and a flush swept across his cheeks as he looked up at her.

"Hey there, Evie," he said with hesitation. She read guilt all over Mike's face.

A part of her wanted to hate him for firing Finch, but she couldn't. He was a good man who valued family over everything else. She knew that if there were threats against his thriving business, he'd always put his family first even if that meant doing the wrong thing, like firing Finch.

"Hey, Mike," she said, trying to garner a smile.

He heaved himself up off of the ground and wiped his hands against his grimy pants. He adjusted the knob on the radio and said, "I was real sorry to let Finch go." He shook his head and gave her a sad look.

"That's why I've come here."

He took off his cap and moved his bangs out of his tanned face.

"I need to know who came to your place to ask you to fire him," she said.

"Why, Evie?" he asked in a strained voice, one that evoked more pain from his end. She knew the whole ordeal got to him, and for that she was grateful. A little bit of hurt made her feel better, even though she knew it shouldn't have.

"I want to talk to them is all," she said nonchalantly, forcing a shrug to make it seem like she couldn't care less.

"Well…" he started with a stutter. He shifted on his feet and rubbed his thumbs against his index fingers.

"I just want to talk with them and see if they'll listen to me about Finch."

He breathed in and exhaled. "I don't know if you can reason with 'em, Evie."

She waited for him to tell her. Something. For him to spew out a few names. All she needed was a name or two.

"I can't do it, Evie," he finally said.

A line formed across her forehead. "Why?"

"'Cause it ain't going to do you any good. It ain't just a few of them, Evie."

"I'll go to every person's house and set them straight. Just give me a list," she said, knowing that she sounded like a mad woman on some strange vengeance mission.

"I can't, and like I said to Finch, it'll blow over eventually. People forget and move on."

Evie knew the people well enough in her town to know that they wouldn't just get over it. They'd hold onto their hatred and ignorant beliefs for as long as they lived and had an audience cheering them on.

"Sorry," he added.

"Thanks anyway, Mike. I'll see you later," she said. She spun on her heels and added, "One of them was McDaniels, right?" She checked his reaction, seeing that his shifting eyes gave her the answer she already knew.

"Humph," she muttered. "Bet he was the ring leader."

"Just leave it be, Evie. You ain't going to reason with McDaniels," he called out to her as she left.

She felt a shift in the wind as she headed to her truck. The air was moist and thick with humidity. Even though it was fall, a hurricane from the south had impacted the weather, and made it temperamental and warm, like a summer's day. The sky was dark, and Evie looked up and saw the sun was hidden by a sheet of gray clouds. The trees ruffled. Their limbs swayed, and the one street light in Haines moved precariously against the wind. The wire it was attached to seemed so frail as it careened against the wild gusts. Birds perched low on telephone wires and sought their prey. Ducks moved in formation, going further south.

It had been a good long while since she'd stepped foot on Nate McDaniels' property, possibly a year—she didn't know for sure. She rarely went over there, and as she grew older the more she was inclined to stay away. McDaniels always made her feel uncomfortable, and Katie's mom always seemed to be nervous. She was a kind woman with a good heart, but someone can only stand under a rain cloud for so long until it drenches her.

She always hated their house. It was flashy and gaudy. Nate had torn down the pretty little farm house that was on the property and rebuilt it with a gargantuan Antebellum house that belonged out on some plantation further south and not in the middle of farm country in the upstate of South Carolina. His land wasn't anything to covet either. Most of the soil wasn't fertile, and his cows were always thinner than most of the other cattle in the area. Evie knew for sure she'd never want to eat any of the meat he was selling. She knew he skimped on things and had heard a tale or two about cows getting sick from moldy hay and poor diet. He didn't see the need to give them vitamins. It was the bare minimum with him.

She parked her truck and walked up the front steps. The rocking chairs moved with the wind, and her blonde locks blew in her face. She tugged her hair behind her ears and tapped on the front door. Julia, Katie's mom, answered with a subtle smile. Things were awkward between them. Evie figured the woman felt guilt and knew that she was doing wrong concerning Katie. A mother had to feel some type of remorse for kicking out her pregnant daughter, or at least for allowing her husband to.

"Evie," she said with a question. More like, what in the world are you doing here?

"Mrs. McDaniels." She never called her Julia like she had insisted. There wasn't a bond between the two, and the one time Evie had tried it, it felt foreign on the tip of her tongue. "Is your husband here?"

"He is," she said, still giving her that questioning look.

"I'd like to speak with him if I can."

"Is Katie okay?" She moved forward and a look of concern flickered in her tired eyes.

"She's fine."

"I..." she started but seemed to be holding back.

Evie didn't say anything and just stared at her. She figured that was best in a situation like this. She wasn't going to offer her any sympathy, and she wasn't going to berate her either. She knew most of what had been done to Katie was from Nate's hands, and Julia was just one of his puppets.

"I miss her," she blurted.

"She misses you, too," Evie said.

"I think about her."

"You should come over and see her."

She slowly shook her head. "I can't," she whispered.

"Well, that's a shame because I know she'd love to see you."

Julia's eyes filled with tears. "He's in his office." She opened the door wider and motioned for Evie to come in. "I'll go get him."

Evie thought their house had a strange scent. Like fresh peaches and body odor. As soon as you walked in, you were greeted by dead animal heads showcased on one wall and an ugly paint by numbers oil painting on another. Nate had painted the horrific piece of art, and most anyone who saw it cringed. Oil on velvet could make anyone queasy.

Katie always said that the animal heads gave her the creeps. She swore their eyes were following her when she walked around the house. Evie would just laugh her off, but standing there and looking into their glass eyes, she saw why Katie thought that. A cold shiver thumbed its way up her spine. There wasn't a lot of light in the house. The curtains were mostly drawn in all of the rooms, and what little light there was wasn't enough to make the home feel cheery. It felt more like a lodge, a place where men would sit around and drink brandy and smoke cigars and talk about nothing that mattered. It screamed Nate and all the things he liked, and Evie saw there wasn't much of Julia in the home—or of Katie for that matter.

Even Katie's bedroom felt that way. Evie always thought that there wasn't much of Katie in that room with the exception of her blue vanity that they had repainted together one afternoon and the wall filled with posters of Steve McQueen. Evie teased Katie for having those posters. "He's too old for you," she'd say, and Katie would just shrug and say, "He's gorgeous." Evie was beginning to understand that her best friend may have a penchant for older men. Preston wasn't fresh out of high school, and Katie wouldn't admit it, but she was definitely attracted to him.

She rocked on her heels, trying hard not to look up at the glass eyes staring down at her. Poor deer, she thought. She knew McDaniels threw out the meat and used his kill as trophies. She just hated the waste of it all. At least when her daddy and Cooper went hunting, they ate what they hunted. There wasn't ever a scrap of meat left.

She sat down and sank bank into the leather chair. It smelled like whiskey and had a faint odor of cigars. She crinkled her nose and took in the room. For a farmer, Nate had expensive things. She always wondered where in the world he got all of his money. Julia had money when they married, but not that much. Not so much that he could afford to buy a new toy or gadget or truck whenever it suited him. He tired of things as quickly as he got them. And women were the same. She'd heard about him sleeping around town, shacking up with women for a short spell only to move onto the next. Evie figured her mom was one of the few he'd never grown tired of. Maybe because they were kindred spirits: two lonely, selfish souls destined to make each other miserable.

"Evelyn," McDaniels said as he entered the room. Julia scooted out immediately, leaving the two of them alone.

He sat down and hitched his feet up on the coffee table, putting his hands behind his head and looking up at Evie with a smug expression. A toothpick dangled outside the corner of his mouth and the first few buttons to his shirt was unbuttoned. Gray hairs sprinkled out. Evie was repulsed, thinking he thought he was the stuff, and she saw at one time he was a good looking man, but him flaunting what wasn't there just made her even more disgusted by him.

"I saw your mother," he said.

"I did, too." She wondered why her mother had even bothered to see him since he'd basically dumped her when she found out she was pregnant with Emily. But she wasn't going to ask him that question. It'd show curiosity, and the last thing she wanted him to think was that she cared.

"Well, if you're here to get money from me for that kid, it won't happen."

"I don't want your money." She tried to maintain a poker face, one that wouldn't show him just how irritated she really was, how much his words, his actions really irked her. "She's not yours anyhow."

He raised a brow and said with a smirk, "You keep on believing that. Rebecca could sell land east of the Everglades. There's no way she was sleeping with your daddy when she was with me."

"You go on thinking that," Evie said, playing off his words. Nate wasn't amused and scowled at her. "She looks just like Daddy. She has his eyes, his nose." She studied his face and said with a haughty tone, "Nope. Not a speck of resemblance between you two."

"Age sure caught up with her. Guess you can see how things are going to turn out for you in twenty years. Can't be pretty and young forever," he said with a twisted lip. "And for women who don't have much else it sure is a big disappointment."

"Age catches up to everyone." She narrowed her eyes to his. "And some people are born ugly and get uglier the older they get."

He laughed forcefully. "Always were a spitfire, just like your mother." He fiddled with his hair. "She came to tell me that the girl wasn't mine and to leave her be. I told her that she was wasting her breath because even if she was mine, I wasn't going to claim her anyway. Last thing I want to do is raise another ungrateful wretch."

"You can't claim a human being, and she's better off without you anyway," Evie snapped and then quickly recovered, remembering why she came over there in the first place. She had to stay calm. If he knew he was already crawling under her skin, he'd keep going after her until he trapped her like the animals he hunted.

"If you're here about my Katie, save your breath. I'm through with her." He took his feet off of the coffee table and stood up. "I was done with her the moment she got knocked up and moved in with you."

"If I recall, she didn't have any other choice than to move in with me," Evie shot back. "'Sides, she's better off now." She paused for a moment and then said, "I want to know why you're spreading rumors about Finch." She was staying put in that oversized chair until she got her answer.

He placed his hands on his hips. "I'm just telling people the truth: he's a lowlife carny who needs to go back to wherever in the hell he came from. We don't need people like him tainting our good town."

That was another thing Evie always noticed about McDaniels. He cursed around women, and Gray always told Evie that a true gentleman will hold his tongue around a lady.

She stood up and pointed her finger at him. "You don't know anything about him. I know you're responsible for the fire and the carnival accident, and because of who you are, you'll get away with it. But know this," she moved closer to him and glared up at him, "he's not going anywhere, and eventually everyone will see through your lies."

He let out another exaggerated laugh and leaned over her. "If you really thought that way, you wouldn't be over here begging me to leave him alone, and if he was a man he wouldn't have his girl doing all his dirty work."

"If you were a real man you wouldn't treat your daughter or wife the way you do." The fire in her belly was growing. She didn't know where this surge of strength came from, but even though she heard her heart hammering against her chest and her legs were having a hard time staying still, she felt grounded. "I know why you covet Daddy's land. It's not just because it's better than this," she spat, spreading her arms out wide, "no, it's because you've always hated him for being a good man, which is something you aren't and won't ever be. And you know that! Deep inside that cold callous heart of yours, you know that you'll never be half the man he was, and you can't stand it."

He brought his fist up to her chin and stared at her with venom.

"Go on and get before I forget that I don't hit women."

"Leave us alone and wallow in your own misery," she shouted back. Who cares that his fist was centimeters from her left cheek. Let him hit her, she thought. Then she could tell the whole damn town and maybe they'd wake up and see him for what he was: a venomous snake. "You're a horrible person. The Devil's got a place in hell waiting for you!"

She turned on her heels and walked to the front door, taking one last glance over her shoulder, seeing the hatred in his eyes. She heard him breathing. His chest rose and then fell flat. He impatiently tapped his fingers against his jeans, like he was debating running after her and punching her in the face.

"Get!" he hollered. "Before I come over there and slap that smirk right off!"

She pushed the front door open and headed to her truck. She had to catch her breath, and her hands wouldn't stop shaking. Her legs felt like jelly, all wobbly and unsteady, and her skin was cold and clammy. She struggled to get the key in the ignition. She sat on her hands for a minute and took a deep breath, hoping it'd quell the uneasiness that filled her. She felt her heart rate calm and her legs weren't moving up and down anymore. As she turned the ignition, she looked toward the McDaniels' house and saw Julia staring at her through her window. She gestured with her fingers, pointing down and to the side. Evie glanced and saw a folded note addressed to Katie sitting on the passenger side of her truck. She nodded at Julia and slowly drove off.

CHAPTER 15

The sky grew darker as Evie made her way back home. Even the bright light from her truck's headlights didn't offer much reprieve from the blackness surrounding her. The Myers' front lawn was full of preteens playing games and doing things kids their age would, she supposed. She'd never cared for Logan, but now that she knew he was the one behind all the hateful graffiti on her barn and her cow, she liked him a lot less. Blue balloons tied to the mail box flapped in the wind, and a hand painted sign that read "Logan's 14th Birthday Party" was staked in the ground below it. It wasn't enough that they threw a party, they wanted the whole town to know that the squirt was turning a year older. Big deal, she thought.

She drove toward her house and noticed the calves were laying down. She remembered what her daddy always said: "Cows know when a storm is coming. They lay down. You ever see them laying down when it ain't night time, you better run for shelter."

When he said that, she chalked it up to urban legend. He was notorious for exaggerating. He'd told her when she was a kid that when she died, her hair would be sold and placed on doll's heads. She was too young at the time to realize that her flaxen hair would be gray when she passed and cried at such a notion. She wasn't vain about her hair; she just didn't want someone touching it after she died. "I'm dead so they need to leave me be!" she had hollered, and Gray just laughed.

"I'm just getting your goat is all," he had told her.

Now as Evie watched the calves huddled together laying in the grass, she wondered if her daddy was full of bunk. So much of what he knew about cows was spot on, and she was thankful she'd learned from a master. Mr. Jacobs, who she sold the cows to after they'd birthed their calves and who owned the most lucrative dairy farm in the upstate, had told her, "You've got the healthiest dairy cows in the upstate, Evie. I don't know what your secret is, but I sure would like to have you working for me."

She'd just smiled and laughed it off, but the offer was intriguing. Getting paid real money to tell someone simple stuff she'd picked up along the way and had picked up from her daddy and her granddaddy before him. And from the look of Mr. Jacobs' face, she knew he wasn't just being kind. He was a business man and wanted to earn a big profit. Having healthy, robust cows producing milk was money in the bank for him. "You give that some thought," he told her on her way out, and that's what she'd done for the past couple of weeks.

Rain drops fell against her windshield. Her wipers moved in a slow rhythm, to the beat of a dance tune meant for lovers. By the time they swooshed to one side, droplets of rain covered the glass, impeding her ability to see anything further than a few feet away. She trudged slowly, aiming to get home before she got stuck out there on that dirt road.

Tree branches swayed, and the wind whistled. Evie pulled into her long driveway. The barn doors flapped—the lock hardly kept the two heavy wooden doors from swinging wide open. She opened her door, greeted by the heavy rain, and she rushed to the porch, drenched by the time she got there.

Katie opened the door and gave her a worried frown. "We were worried."

"It's just rain is all," Evie said, wiping off the drops of water from her shoulder to her wrist. A small puddle had formed on her floors.

She reached into her pocket and pulled out the damp folded piece of paper. "This is for you."

Katie peered down at it and showed a look of recognition. "It's from Momma."

Evie nodded.

"Is that where you were?" she asked.

"Yes. I went to talk some sense into your dad," Evie confessed. "About Finch."

"Well, that was a useless mission, wasn't it?"

"Yeah," Evie sighed and decided to say nothing more about the subject. It proved to be a fruitless task, but at least she was able to get her two cents in about him. At least she told him where to stick it. She had a slew of things to spew out at him given the time.

There wasn't any use in stating the obvious, going into detail about what a scumbag McDaniels had proven himself to be. Katie knew her father was a good for nothing.

Evie left a trail of muddy footprints as they made their way back to the kitchen.

"Good Lord, Eves, you're a mess," Katie said, pointing to the floor.

Evie glanced over her shoulder and gave an apologetic shrug. "I'm just like Daddy." She smiled to herself. All that time she'd bickered at him for leaving a mess around the house and now that's what she was doing. Things sure did come full circle, she thought.

Finch gave her a relieved smile and stood up, wiping off the water on Evie's arms. "I thought we were going to have to send a search party after you." He tugged on her wet hair.

"That rain gets any worse, we're going to have to haul the cows into the barn," she said. She looked out the window and slightly frowned.

"Where've you been?" he asked.

"In town taking care of business," she answered vaguely. Finch raised an eyebrow. He was onto her, and she'd end up confessing in a matter of time anyway.

She glanced down at her little sister, who was toying with her food. She tried to offer a smile. "You eatin' good?" That was all Evie could think to say. Man, she felt pathetic, like those novices who thought cows were cute and would just say, "Ain't he cute?" when they'd come over to her farm and swoon over the six-hundred pound beasts.

Mothering wasn't going to be easy, she figured. And trying to say the right thing was going to be a stretch. How'd she know what the right words were? How'd she know when she was doing right?

"Yes," Emily said. She twirled the spaghetti around her fork.

"That looks good," Evie said. She was trying, like couples on a first date out for dinner who had nothing in common but kept the conversation going because it'd only been twenty minutes and the food hadn't been served yet.

Emily just kept playing with her food. Finch gave Evie a look, the kind that told her to hang in there.

"Anyone home?" Doris shouted.

"We're in here!" Finch called back.

Doris' heavy steps vibrated against the wood floors; the small pitter-pattering of Mouse's feet paled in comparison. A squish and squeak were heard as they padded their way to the kitchen.

Friedrich, Mouse and Doris entered the kitchen, soaked and out of breath. Mouse took off his fedora and a puddle of water fell to the floor. His wool trousers looked like heavy weights, and he yanked on his suspenders, trying to pull them up. Friedrich moved his wet hair away from his face, and Doris' blue eye shadow washed down her cheeks. Her pink frock suctioned against her hefty body.

"Honey Lamb, those cows are gonna drown out there," she said to Evie.

Mouse placed his palm against his right hip and grimaced. Some years back, while on the circuit, he'd fallen off the stage and landed on his hip. The damage became permanent after a near fatal beating from an ignorant townie sent him to the hospital for a week. Brittle bones and old age had made it worse in the past year.

"They won't drown," Evie said. She glanced out the window and noticed a thick black cloud covered the sky. Wind chimes clattered, jostled by the heavy winds. "We'll have to haul them in the barn till this blows over." She brought her hand to her mouth and chewed on a nail.

"That is why we are here. Those calves cannot survive this," Friedrich said.

"Poor cows," Mouse added.

"I can't believe y'all walked over here in this weather," Evie said.

"It wasn't this bad when we left to come here, Honey Lamb."

"It just came out of nowhere," Evie said. She walked to the kitchen counter and turned on the radio. After she adjusted the knob, she turned up the volume, and everyone grew quiet.

"Severe thunderstorms likely across the upstate today. A storm will approach from the south, bringing showers and thunderstorms with possible flash flooding in Greenville, Anderson, and Oconee Counties. Temperatures will warm, creating an unstable air mass. Wind speeds could be damaging and tornados and hail will be possible. Everyone in the Upstate is strongly encouraged to hunker down until this storm

passes."

Evie turned the volume down and twisted her lips to the side. "Well... shit."

"It looks like tornado weather." Friedrich pointed out the window. "I experienced a few when I was on the circuit."

"We don't get them up here that often, but that storm front is causing all of this crazy weather," Evie said. "We better get the cows under shelter till this passes." She chewed off a loose nail and bit hard on her lip. Blood covered the ends of her two front teeth. She turned to face Katie. "You stay in here with Emily and gather up candles, matches, and flash lights. I'm thinking we're not going to have power later on tonight."

Katie nodded and started searching for those items. "You stay in here with Katie, okay?" Evie said to Emily, trying to soften up her tone.

"I can help you," Emily said.

"I know, but this weather is too moody," she said.

"Okay," Emily sighed.

Evie noticed Finch's eyes brightened, and he held his smile. He'd already told her on more than one occasion they were similar spirits.

"Let's go." She pushed the door open, and it swung even further from the wind. She lowered her head, fighting the hard rain, and moved her way toward the barn.

Friedrich and Finch grabbed onto the door handles and pulled the heavy doors open, battling the wind. Everyone hurried inside, and they slammed the doors shut.

"Finch, Mouse and Doris, y'all stand near the feeding barn and help call them in. Friedrich and me will haul them in," Evie said. She was commanding the room. Her small, five foot frame wasn't an issue. When it came to cattle, they all listened to her. She was the voice of authority.

She hopped on her ATV; Friedrich did the same. Finch opened the doors, and a gust of wind blew through the barn. Doris, Mouse and Finch made their way down to the feeding barn as Evie and Friedrich rode near the huddled cattle.

"Sug! Sug!" she shouted. Friedrich mimicked her, hollering at the top of his lungs.

They raised their arms in the air and motioned toward the barn, shouting at the scared, wet cattle.

One by one the cattle trickled into the barn, with Finch, Mouse and Doris maneuvering them inside. Their bodies juxtaposed—they whined and mooed—and Finch felt a tinge of sadness seeing their frightened eyes as they made their way into the barn.

Evie kept wiping at her face, but the rain was pouring down on her, and she couldn't see what was in front of her. She saw a glimpse of a beast off in the far corner of her property and drove toward the speck of brown, hoping that her ATV didn't fumble over a rock or something else. It was like driving in fog. She drove slowly, trying hard to keep her eyes open, but the rain was falling hard. "Sug!" she shouted! "Sug! Sug!" The calf mooed and went to the right. Evie followed closely behind it, trying to get it to keep moving forward. Her voice was growing hoarse from screaming, and the engine was becoming water logged. The clay soil was getting softer, muddier, and the wheels on her ATV were spinning round and round but moving a centimeter at a time.

She pushed the accelerator forward and the ATV took off, faster than she'd anticipated. She sped down hill and pulled hard on the brake, but the ATV was out of control and wouldn't slow down. She pumped the hand brake over and over. Blinded by the rain, Evie couldn't tell which direction she was headed, and as she reached the bottom of the hill, the ATV shot upward and over, with Evie still on it.

Evie heard what sounded like a twig snapping in half, and then she realized that it wasn't a twig and that the sound came from her. It hurt to breathe, and she didn't have the strength to get the ATV off of her.

CHAPTER 16

Friedrich had come back, but there was no sign of Evie. Finch grew worried and jumped on Friedrich's ATV, sitting behind him as they drove up the hill. The ATV struggled to gain momentum. The ground was flooding, and the soil was soft and mushy.

"What's over there?" Finch yelled to Friedrich.

Friedrich headed over in the direction that Finch pointed. Once they were close enough, Finch saw it was Evie and that her ATV was laying directly on top of her. He hurried off the moving ATV and dashed to her.

"Evie," he said with concern. Friedrich reached them and let the ATV idle as he hopped off to help Finch lift the heavy machine.

Together they heaved the machine off of Evie as she quietly whimpered from the mounting pressure. Evie wasn't one to complain and could usually tolerate pain. When she was a little girl, she fell from a tree and broke her arm. She never shed a tear, and she wasn't about to cry from a few cracked ribs.

Finch bent down, wiped the water off of her face and pushed her hair back so he could look in her blue eyes. "Can you walk?" he asked in gentle tone. It scared the hell out of him when he saw her lying there with the ATV on top of her. He thought the worst, and for a split second, a feeling of emptiness filled him. His life would be nothing without Evie in it. He'd never worried for her safety, for her life, until that second, and once he got to her, all he wanted to do was cradle her in his arms and keep her safe and sound.

She wiggled her toes and moved her legs slightly, enough to know that they were not broken. She let out a cough and brought her arms up to her chest. "Yeah," she said. He extended his hand and helped her up.

She moaned from the movement, and he gave her a worried frown. Hail started to fall. The sharp stinging pain from the pellets were beating them up. The contact was like being pricked with pin needles piercing into their skin.

"That does not look good," Friedrich said, pointing up. A thick band of clouds had joined together, creating a large black mass covering most of the sky. Lightning flashed, like the crack of a whip, and hail continued to pummel them.

Finch had experienced a tornado or two during his years in the carnival. He'd spent some time in tornado alley, dodging bad storms and hunkering down in flimsy tents not built to survive a thunderstorm. He remembered one time when he and his mom huddled together underneath one of the trailers, praying to God that they'd make it. It was one of the few times in his life he'd ever been frightened, and he could still remember hearing the sound of the wind howl— like a train was coming— and the feel of the earth shaking above and beneath him.

He gave Friedrich a serious look, and said, "We need to get inside." He helped Evie to the ATV and had her sit behind Friedrich.

"Finch, get on!" she yelled.

"There's no room," he said.

Her forehead wrinkled. "You can't go back on foot."

"I can run," he said and shouted to Friedrich, "Better get going!"

Friedrich raced off like a bandit. Finch took one look at the sky and saw the mass of black clouds had started to funnel. He started to run, praying that he'd make it inside their house before the tornado came his way.

He ran faster than he ever had. His lungs felt as if they were going to burst, and his heart was beating wildly. He looked up in the sky and saw the tornado was jumping from one place to the next. Landing in one location, unleashing its wrath and destroying whatever was in its way before it moved on to another location. He knew the kind. The small tornadoes were the ones to worry about. Hell, every tornado was worth worrying about. But the small ones were quick and were prone to move from one place to the next within a matter of seconds. He was struggling to run against the wind. Each passing moment felt as if he was being pulled back by a large elastic band. He pushed on with all of his might. He swung his arms back and forth and took deep breaths as his legs moved swiftly in motion.

He pushed the kitchen door open and shut it behind him. "Where's?" He bent over and caught his breath. "Evie."

"She's upstairs. Doris is taping her up. She thinks she broke a few ribs," Mouse said. He patted himself with a hand towel, drying off remnants of rain.

Friedrich glanced out the window. "We need to get in the bathroom. Now!"

A mass of whirling black clouds was coming their way. It sounded as if three semi trucks hoarding a herd of cattle had trampled up the driveway. An eerie silence pervaded the room. The hairs on Finch's arms stood up even though he was sweating. He felt a chill come over him despite the warmth and humidity in the air.

"Right now," Friedrich said in a calm tone.

"Evie!" Finch said and dashed out of the room and up the stairs. "Evie!" He pushed the bathroom door wide open and said in a hurried tone, "We need to get in the downstairs bathroom."

Evie sat on the bathtub in nothing but her bra and underwear while Doris wrapped masking tape around her midsection. Normally, Finch would have ogled at the site, but this wasn't the time and that was the furthest thing from his mind.

"A tornado is coming!" he shouted frantically. He grabbed Evie's pink chenille housecoat off of the door hook and wrapped it around her. She struggled to get her arms in the holes and slowly stood up. He wrapped the tie around her small waist and said, "I'm going to carry you."

"Lawd have mercy, Finch. I can walk," she said, pushing him away from her, but he wouldn't budge. He grabbed her and gently lifted her up, cradling her in his arms. Katie took Emily by the hand and shot out of the room. Doris followed close behind as they headed downstairs and huddled in the bathroom with Friedrich and Mouse.

Evie moaned, and Finch whispered, "I know it hurts. I'm sorry." He quickened his pace downstairs, jostling Evie as he made each step. She winced from the impact and bit down hard on her lip.

"Never broken a rib before, but man does it hurt," she said between shortened breaths. She laughed, then moaned again from the movement. "And my damn ATV is done for, isn't it?"

He shot her a quick smile, amazed by her ability to turn anything into a joke. "I've broken several ribs more than once," he said and figured he'd tell those tales later when they weren't in the midst of danger. "And that ATV was a piece of crap anyway."

Even though he should have been worried, all he thought about was being with her, keeping her safe, and knowing that she was in his arms gave him an overwhelming sense of peace, like everything was going to be okay. All this time he'd worried about the obstacles they'd faced, and now as he held her, he saw none of it mattered. All that was important was in that small bathroom of hers: the people. That was it.

They stood close to each other, hearing every peep that anyone made: a swallow, a gulp, a clearing of the throat. Any noise was amplified by the deafening silence in the room—a room that was too small for all of them. Emily stood in the bathtub with Mouse and Katie. They held hands like they were about to sing "Kumbaya" around a lit campfire.

Finch let Evie down into the bathtub and kissed her hard on the mouth. If this was it, he wanted the last image in his mind to be of her and the last thing he ever felt to be her lips. He'd be happy dying with his lips on hers if that was the way fate wanted it. So long as he had her, death didn't scare him. And Evie didn't fight him. She forgot that there were others in the room. She wanted to feel the touch of his lips on hers—the taste of him. It brought her comfort, knowing that if something happened, if life decided it was done with them, at least the last image that was in her mind was of him.

He held onto her hand, rubbing the surface with his fingers. Friedrich wrapped his arms around Doris' thick waist and brought her close to him, stroking her arms over and over again. Finch wasn't a praying man but at a time like this he said a quick one, hoping that, if anything, Evie was going to be all right. All that mattered was her.

The house began to vibrate, and they heard things falling off of the walls: glass shattering from picture frames; knick knacks and other objects falling to the floor, breaking into shambles. The overhead light flickered, and Emily let out a screech. Katie patted her, trying to soothe her. Evie leaned against Finch's chest, hearing his heart beat frantically. Their breaths increased, and the bathroom grew warm, stifling. The light continued to brighten then dim, and finally the room was pitch black.

No one said a word. Their shallow breaths were the only sound. Finch stood with Evie nestled close to him wondering when they could get out of that bathroom and see if the tornado had caused damage. The floor shook again, and everyone held their breaths.

Emily sniffled and cried quietly, "It's dark in here."

Evie tried to say something sweet, something that'd keep her calm. "We'll only be in here for a little while longer." But even she knew that wasn't necessarily the truth. She had no idea how long she'd be in there: minutes, hours, or even longer. Tornadoes were unpredictable. They could linger for hours, encroaching their fury long enough to leave something that was once beautiful in ruins.

Emily fidgeted. Her tiny arms jerked back and forth. She stepped out of the bathtub. Her feet pressed hard against Finch's as she padded her way in the dark. He tried holding her back but he couldn't see her. Without any window, there wasn't a source of light shining through to guide him. She trudged pass Friedrich and Doris and shoved the door wide open. A burst of light shined on them. They squinted their eyes from the sudden change.

"Emily! No!" Finch warned.

"Come back here!" Evie shouted, but Emily kept moving. "What is she doing?" Evie said to Finch. Evie slowly stepped out of the bathtub and headed toward the open door. Finch tried holding her back but Evie fought him and said, "I can't let her go out there!"

Finch followed Evie, gingerly moving from outside the

bathroom to the hallway. Emily crouched in the kitchen, her back against the pantry door. She cried into her arms and peeked up at them when he called her name.

"Emily," he whispered. He glanced out the window and saw that the sun was peeking through a pillow of clouds.

"I couldn't stand being in that small space. It was so dark," she cried. "So dark," her voice trailed off.

"She's claustrophobic," he whispered to Evie.

Evie tried squatting to the floor to soothe Emily, but the pain was too much. Instead she stood over her, running her fingers through Emily's honeyed locks.

"You're safe now," Evie said to her.

He looked out the window once more and then glanced back at Evie. "The sun's out."

Her eyes shot toward the window. "Already?"

"That's the way these kind of storms work. All hell breaks loose; then it's all sunshine and flowers afterward." He examined outside one more time and then said, "Let me go take a look."

"No," Evie warned, but it fell on deaf ears. Finch was already half-way out the door.

Debris had fallen in various places. Tree limbs had blown off or were barely hanging on and would soon tear off with any gust of wind. The house appeared to be okay, and when he cupped his palm over his eyes, he saw that the cattle were all in one piece in the barn. The roof was still intact, and all of the other structures looked fine. He breathed a sigh of relief, thanking the stars above that at least her land had been salvaged. At least the house and everyone in it had been spared. He opened the door and gave a faint smile to Evie. "Everything looks okay."

"I need to check on my cows," she said, dropping her fingers away from Emily's head and to her side. "You okay?"

Emily nodded and gave her a grateful smile. She reached her hand out to Evie, and Evie clasped onto it and held it tight. "We got you, okay?" Evie said. "We've always got you."

Still holding Evie's hand, Emily stood up. The effort was too much for Evie, and a look of pain shot across her face from the movement. "Guess I gotta take it easy." She grunted under her breath.

Finch called to Doris, Mouse, Katie and Friedrich in the bathroom. "You can come out!" He lifted the phone off of the receiver. "Phone's dead."

"We probably won't have power for a while. Last time we had a bad storm, it took two days for them to fix it," Evie said.

Mouse was the first to peer around the corner. He moved hesitantly and looked around from side to side before stepping foot inside of the kitchen. Doris fanned herself. Sweat trickled down her face, and Friedrich squeezed the back of his neck. His jaw was tense and he gave Finch a look of relief. Katie's face was flushed.

"Those cows are most likely frightened," Friedrich said to Evie.

"We've got one ATV and damaged goods." Evie pointed to herself.

"Let's get out there before she bites her lip off," Finch said with a tease. Evie quickly retracted her teeth from her lips and glared at him.

"I wasn't chewing..." She threw her arms up in the air. "Oh, forget it!" She made a pained face and quickly brought her arms to her chest.

He laughed and tugged onto her hand. "If anyone's biting

that lip it's going to be me," he whispered to her and kissed her neck. For a quick second she forget where she was and a trail of goosebumps formed on her clammy skin. All she thought about as she stared into his chocolate brown eyes was kissing him.

Her fingers brushed against her robe's soft chenille threading. "Gotta change first."

"Want me to carry you?" he asked with a wide grin.

"'No," she said. "I can manage."

"Too bad," he said and picked her up off of the ground and cradled her against him.

"Finch!" She tried pushing against him but deep down she liked the idea, any girl with sense would. She couldn't stop staring at his bulging muscles as he carried her up the stairs. He blew his long brown bangs away from his brown eyes and gave her a lovestruck goofy grin.

She leaned close to him and took a whiff, smelling the earth and a faint hint of soap.

"How long are you going to be carrying me around like I'm Scarlett O'Hara?"

"As long as you'll let me. I like having your body near mine," he said with a glint in his eyes. "I love you so much, Evie. If you'll just shut up and let me love you, you'll see I'll do this and more." He gently set her down on her bedroom floor. "I've got a bag of tricks up my sleeve guaranteed to make you swoon." He formed a lopsided grin and started to close the door behind him.

"Finch!"

He cracked the door open and peeped inside her room.

"The sooner we get married, the better. I love you, you know?"

"I know, but it's nice to hear." He shut the door behind him.

***

Friedrich and Finch rode on the ATV surveying the land while Evie let the cows out of the barn. Every one of them was fine, just shaken up by the weather and timid and scared from all of the racket the storm had caused. Evie tried to use a gentle voice to steer them out of the barn, but some were still too petrified to move outside.

"Sug! Sug!" she shouted, and then folded her arm against her chest, feeling an instant shooting pain. It hurt to move, and her chest had expanded from the cracked ribs. "Come on," she whispered to the cattle. "It's okay. I promise."

The cows moved a few steps and finally let loose out of the barn and onto the pasture, like a preacher's son dropped off on a college campus with no adult supervision. Evie watched as Finch and Friedrich rode up and down the hill on the one working ATV. Just another thing to add to the list, she thought. Now she'd have to buy another one, and that wouldn't be cheap.

As Finch and Friedrich rode up and down the hills, they'd let the ATV idle as they stacked broken tree limbs and move debris off to the side and into small piles.

"This isn't that bad," Friedrich said and Finch agreed. It wasn't. It could have been worse.

Friedrich rode to the side of the property that they shared with the Myers' family. As they inched closer, they noticed their barn roof had caved. The ridge beam had collapsed into the shape of a "v" and the rest of the structure was precariously standing.

Friedrich pointed in that direction, and Finch shouted, "They've been hit!"

Friedrich steered the ATV closer to the property line and turned off the ATV. He and Finch scanned the Myers' property. The tornado hadn't been kind to them. The barn was all but gone, and a tree had fallen on Mr. Myers' pick up truck – the windshield was cracked and the hood was dented in. They saw their house off in the distance: strips of wood siding had peeled off the structure, and some of the roof was gone.

"This is terrible," Friedrich said.

Finch nodded in agreement and then thought how fortunate they had been that the tornado hadn't made a bee line for them.

Friedrich glanced down at the bottom of the wooden fence that separated the property and saw that pieces of "Logan's birthday" sign were tattered and spread across the wet grassy lawn. Deflated blue balloons lay off in the distance. One lone balloon bounced on the ground. The attached curled ribbon dragged along the grass as it moved from one spot to the next.

Finch turned his head in the direction of the barn. "You hear that?"

A faint moaning filled the air, and then as Finch and Friedrich stopped talking, they heard screaming. Friedrich gave Finch a sudden look of horror.

"The children!"

CHAPTER 17

Friedrich hopped over the fence, and Finch followed. As they ran toward the barn, the shrill sound of children's screams and the echo of sobbing grew louder and louder.

Friedrich shot Finch a worried look as they moved close to the barn. The second story had caved into the first floor. The walls stood jagged and leaned against each other. Strips of wood lay off in the grass, and bales of hay were spread amongst the destruction.

"Hello! Hello!" Friedrich shouted into the crumbled barn.

"Help!" a woman shouted.

"We're here to help you," Friedrich said.

"Help us!" she shouted again.

"Try not to worry. We'll get you out," he said in a calm voice. "How many of you are in there?"

"Eight. My husband, he's..." her voice faded and she sniffled. "And my son, Logan," she added. Logan's cries overshadowed her frenzied voice. "His friends are in here." She coughed and moaned.

"Stay calm and don't move. We'll get you out," Friedrich said. He turned to Finch and whispered, "We've got to move slowly and carefully. We don't want to make the situation worse."

"Should we go get the others to help?"

"We don't have time for that." Friedrich gave him a sorrowful expression. He made baby steps toward the wreckage, then he bent over and picked up a wooden beam. Finch grabbed the other end, struggling as he lifted the heavy, solid wood off of the pile of destruction.

"Carefully, now," Friedrich instructed with a whisper. His broad chest moved up and down as he carried one end of the wood.

Finch handled the calamity with kid gloves, mimicking Friedrich's movements. The sweat poured from the crown of his head to his face, stinging his brown eyes. His heart rate increased, and he held his breath with each and every step that caused the insecure structure to wobble. One bad move, and they'd all be crushed.

They continued to work quickly, lifting each piece of wood with care. Friedrich tried to soothe their worries. "We'll get you out in a moment," he said. His eyes darted up and to the left and the right. He gave Finch a look.

Finch read him loud and clear. They needed to act fast. The walls and roof were going to give way completely.

Friedrich extended his hand to a preteen boy, whose eyes were closed and teeth were gritted together. Friedrich clasped onto the young boy's hand and lifted him up. "Are you hurt?" he asked.

The boy coughed and held onto his chest. "It hurts."

"Can you walk?"

The boy nodded. "I think so."

He gestured to Finch, who took the boy's hand and led him off far enough away from the wreckage and sat him down.

"We'll have to drive them to the hospital. The phone lines are dead," Finch said.

They continued their task, removing the debris as quickly as they could.

Finch helped Mrs. Myers up. Her eyes were welled with tears. "My son...my husband," she said frantically. Her sandy brown hair was blood-soaked, and her shoulder was dislocated. Just looking at it made Finch wince. He sat her down next to the other boy as he worked in haste to help Friedrich.

The ridge beam rattled. "Hurry!" Friedrich commanded. Any sudden movement could cause it to tumble like Samson when he brought the walls down.

One by one, they dug deeper into the carnage, taking the young boys off to safety. Mr. Myers lay half-unconscious as Friedrich lifted his stout body and carried him to his wife.

"Tate! Tate!" she cried, as Friedrich lay him down in front of her He barely blinked and murmured, "Logan."

She rolled him toward her, cradled him in her arms and brought his head up to her heart. Blood stains covered his Wrangler jeans and green t-shirt. He closed his eyes and blacked out. She shook his lifeless body as his eyes remained closed and his body stayed still. "Tate! Tate!" She placed her head against his chest. "His heart's still beating." She sighed with relief, then began to cry once more. "My boy." She looked up to Friedrich with desperation. "Logan's still in there!"

Like a tree falling in the forest, the sound of timber toppling over filled the atmosphere. Finch looked at Friedrich with wide eyes and an open mouth.

"Logan!" Mrs. Myers screamed, her voice hoarse. She tried standing up but fell back against the ground in agony.

Friedrich leapt to the wreckage. He squatted and heaved the ridge beam up, placing it on his shoulders. He clenched his jaw and shouted to Finch, "Get him out!"

Finch dug through the debris, scouring below the surface for Logan. He saw his arm and pulled on it, the wood piled on top of him shifted as Finch tugged hard on his body. Friedrich breathed heavy and panted. His legs shook. He reached up to adjust the ridge beam, and he moaned, a loud grunt came from him. "Hurry," he breathed.

Finch cleared the area and grabbed Logan by the waist as he dragged his lifeless body out from underneath it all. He placed his head against his chest and heard a subtle heart beat. "He's alive," he said with a relieved grin. He turned to face Friedrich, and his face fell. Friedrich's tattooed face was beet red. His breaths were hard and heavy. He collapsed to the ground, with the ridge beam pressing against his neck.

Finch ran to him and tried to lift it off of him but it was too heavy. Friedrich fought for air and whispered, "Get them to the hospital."

"Freddy!" He cried as he fought with all of his might to get the beam off of him.

The beam remained planted against the back of Friedrich's thick neck, and the sound of his breaths came to a halt. He was suffocating, and there was nothing Finch could do to make it stop. Friedrich's eyes were open but were lost, staring off into space, lifeless. The glint was gone, and all that was left was a shell of the man who Finch considered a father, a hero, a man worthy of his respect. Finch fell down and wailed.

He tried in vain to lift the beam, but it was too much for him. Friedrich had the strength of an elephant, of a superhero, of twenty men or more. He struggled over and over and finally gave up. He touched Friedrich's cold hand, blinking back tears from his eyes. He stared down at his friend and wiped at his wet eyes, feeling another hole forming in his heart.

He heard whimpering. He couldn't stay there all day. They had to get to the hospital. Fast. And they weren't going to die in vain. No one else was dying that day.

He stood up. His knees wobbled, and his breaths were shaky. He lifted Logan off of the ground and carried him to the other injured.

"The hospital." He panted. His eyes were still damp with tears.

"Use my truck," she answered.

His eyes darted to the truck with the broken windshield.

"It's over there." She barely lifted her arm, pointing to her house. "My keys are inside."

He ran as fast as he could, pushing through the pain, the hollow feeling in his heart from the loss of his dear friend. The further he ran, the faster he went, the more the hurt consumed him. He howled, crying as he ran, hating life, hating the world for being so damn unfair. What little he'd been given in life was always taken away. The other voice told him to be thankful that Evie was still in his life, but he found it hard to be grateful. First his mom, now Friedrich. Too quickly in his life he had learned about loss and suffering, and now as he jetted across their pasture, he hated everyone in the Myers family. He hated them with all of his heart for being helpless, for being hurt and needing their help. He blamed them and thought about turning around and running the other way, away from them. A part of him wished that he and Friedrich had no souls. That they wouldn't have taken the risk and had just done what most people would have in that situation: called for help and washed their hands of the perilous circumstance. But that wasn't Friedrich, and if Finch wanted to emulate anyone in his life, it'd be him. He couldn't turn away from those in need, and as he dashed to the truck, all he could think about was getting them to the hospital, even if a small part of him resented them for being alive.

The keys lay on the dash. Finch tried to get them in the ignition, but his hands were trembling. He held onto one hand with the other and shoved it in the ignition. The engine roared, and Finch stepped on the gas, speeding to them as quickly as the truck could go on wet ground. He dodged debris, yanking the truck steering wheel from side to side as he maneuvered around, trying to keep from hitting anything. The last thing he needed was a broken down vehicle.

He let the truck idle as he lifted Logan off of the ground and lay him inside of the truck. Mrs. Myers slowly got up and offered her hand to the other children. Mr. Myers had gained consciousness and nearly stumbled his way to the truck bed. He lay in Mrs. Myers' arms as the children around her wiped at their damp eyes and gave Finch a scared look.

He shut the truck bed and sat down, racing off of their property. The hospital was in Chester, the next town over from Haines, far enough away that time was against them. Finch looked at Logan and wondered if he was going to pull through. "Dammit! You better make it!" he said to him. "He won't die for nothing!" He punched the steering wheel and pressed his foot harder against the gas, weaving on the debris-filled roads as he sped to the hospital.

***

Evie slowly made her way outside, cupping her hand over her eyes. It'd been a while, and they weren't back. Something didn't feel right, and a little voice told her she should worry. She marched back inside and searched for her truck keys.

"Where is Friedrich?" Doris asked.

"I'm going to look for them," Evie said. "Maybe the ATV broke down."

"I'll go with you," Mouse offered and followed her outside.

Doris stood out on the front porch and shouted, "You tell ole Friedrich he's a bad man for making me worry like this."

"Will do!" Evie said and got up inside the truck, holding one arm against her chest as she sat down.

Mouse sat next to her and stared out the window. His brows furrowed, and he frowned. "Seems the tornado decided to take some pity on us."

"About time we were left alone," Evie grumbled.

Evie pressed her foot against the accelerator to give the truck momentum to move up and down the steep hills. Mouse's body shot up from the sudden movement, and Evie clenched her fist against her chest, grunting from the throbbing pain.

She saw the ATV sitting near the border of the Myers' property and hers. She drove the truck toward it and turned it off. Mouse walked with her as she scanned the area. No one was in sight. She searched her neighbor's property and saw the crumbled barn. The sun shined in her eyes, and as she moved in closer, she cupped her hand over them, trying to block it. She took a second look at the destroyed barn, then brought her hand up to her mouth and whispered, "Lawd have mercy." She jumped over the fence and ran through the pain.

She prayed it wasn't Finch. She knew it was selfish to wish death on someone else, making it seem like their life wasn't as precious, but she couldn't handle it if it was him. Finch meant too much to her, and if that meant having those kind of thoughts, then so be it.

She walked carefully on the fallen barn and peered down at Friedrich's lifeless body. She gasped for air and shot Mouse a horrified look.

He placed his hand up to his mouth and shook his head. Tears trickled down from his eyes and he said in a quiet tone, "Too soon."

But even though Evie felt the sadness of seeing her friend lay dead in front of her, all she thought about was Finch: where he was and if he was okay. She quickly searched through the wreckage, hoping to God she wouldn't find him.

Mouse sobbed quietly as Evie rummaged the area. There was a trail of blood, lots and lots of it, enough that more than one person had to have shed it. And she followed to where it led, off to a patch of grass on the pasture, where a big circle of red enveloped an area. She noticed the tire marks in the wet grass and that they led away. Someone had driven off, and if there was that much blood, there was only one place they'd go – the hospital. Her heart skipped a beat and she hurried to her truck.

"We have to go the hospital!" she shouted to Mouse.

"But Friedrich," he said.

"We'll take care of him when we return," she said, softer, hoping to show some respect. She felt awful for not showing enough remorse or sadness, but her heart could only handle so much, and at that moment, her heart ached for Finch.

***

Finch pulled into the Emergency Room drive and kept the truck idling. He rushed inside and shouted to anyone who'd listen. "I have injured people out there!" He pointed to the outside. "Hurry!" He pounded his fist against the counter and shouted again, "Now!"

A few nurses rushed outside with wheelchairs and two followed pushing a gurney. They helped get Mr. and Mrs. Myers out of the back of the truck bed, along with Logan's friends, and had them sit in the wheel chairs. Two of the nurses opened the truck door and eased Logan out and lifted him on top of the gurney.

"Are you hurt?" they asked Finch.

"No," he said. "They were in a barn during the storm, and it fell on them."

They gave him an understanding nod and quickened their pace inside of the hospital. Finch fell back against the truck and brought his hands up to his face. He stood there for a moment, trying to collect himself. He cursed and got into the truck, thinking for that brief moment that he was going to leave. The hell with them, he thought. Who cared if they lived or died? Friedrich was gone, and their lives just weren't as important. He started up the truck and began to drive, but the voice in his head, the one full of reason, shouted at him, telling him to do what was right. Friedrich wouldn't just leave Logan and his family stranded. He'd wait until there was news, until there was certainty. He punched the steering wheel and pursed his lips. He jerked on it and turned around, heading back to the hospital.

He sat down in the waiting room, raking his fingers through his shaggy hair over and over. His legs wouldn't stop moving. The room was packed full of people: crying babies, toddlers pacing the floors, and adults waiting for news, any kind of news.

It felt like hours but may have only been several minutes. Evie marched into the waiting room, searching.

He stood up and said her name. She smiled with relief and ran to him.

"Finch!" she breathed. She held him tight—disregarding her broken ribs—and kissed him. "I thought the worst."

"I'm okay. Friedrich..."

"I know," she whispered. "I saw."

"He saved them," he said and wiped at his eyes. "All of them."

"Are they all right?"

"I don't know. The kid, Logan, he was bad off."

"What do we do?"

"Wait," he said.

CHAPTER 18

They sat for an hour in that hospital waiting room awaiting news about Logan, his family and friends. "It can't be for nothing," Finch said. His knuckles were raw from rubbing against his jeans. His jaw tensed, and his mouth twitched to the side.

Evie touched him on the arm. "You can't think that way or it will kill you."

Despite how mature Finch was, he couldn't help but think that way. This was the kid who was responsible for a lot of hurt and pain. It was only natural for him to harbor resentment because of Friedrich's death.

"You have to let it go, Finch," Mouse murmured.

But Finch was restless and felt lost, like he had when his mother died. He needed direction. He needed Friedrich and didn't realize it until he was gone.

He got up and paced the floor, mimicking the toddlers who were clomping around. He sat down for a moment, then shot back up and walked back and forth in the confining room.

Evie chose not to say anything. He was dealing in his own way. She and Mouse sat quietly, watching as doctors told people the fate of their loved ones.

An older doctor approached them. His white coat was wrinkled, and mustard stained his collar. Long gray hairs curled up at the ends of his bushy eyebrows. He searched the room and approached Finch with hesitation. He tapped Finch on the shoulder. "Are you the young man who brought the Myers family in?"

"Yes," Finch answered. "And his friends."

"They're all going to be fine. Mrs. Myers asked me to tell you," he said, and Evie smiled, as did Mouse. Finch formed a half-smile.

"The boy?" Finch asked. "Logan?"

"He broke several bones and has a slight concussion but should recover quickly. He's lucky you were there to save him."

"I didn't. It was Friedrich Adler. He's the one who save them and died while doing so…" Finch's voice faded.

The doctor frowned and cleared his throat. He looked down at his clip board, fiddling with his ball point pen, clicking it over and over. "If you'll excuse me, I have patients to get back to." He turned on his heels and walked out of the waiting room.

Finch stormed out of the hospital, muttering under his breath and cursing like a fisherman out on turbulent seas. He balled his hand into a fist, and he slammed his knuckles against the concrete wall. Blood splattered, and he hollered in pain.

Evie ran to him and wrapped her arms around him securely. "Finch! Stop!" she screamed desperately. "Stop," she said in a softer voice.

He turned to face her. Tears filled his dark brown eyes. "He was my family."

"I know," she said and pulled him to her. "I know." She held onto him, giving him that moment, that time, to deal with it, to cope, or to at least try.

***

"Think he's okay?" Evie asked Mouse as she drove toward home. Finch sat in the truck bed. He leaned against the rear window. Evie looked in her side mirror and saw his brown hair flying with the wind. He sat with his knees up to his chest and his arms folded over them.

"He just needs time to let it digest. We all do," Mouse said.

"Life isn't fair."

He laughed, and she made a strange face.

He stared down at his short legs, which barely dangled over the truck seat. "Mama used to say that about me. That life was unfair to me, but I was always fine with who I was. She was the one who cared how tall I was going to be."

"My daddy shouldn't have died. My mother never should have deserted Emily, and Friedrich, he should still be alive," Evie said.

"Everyone is supposed to die, Evie, at one point in time. It's just how you look at things. Like my height. I like being small, but my mama didn't like me being small." He breathed heavy, took off his fedora and rubbed the top of his balding head. "Your daddy lived a full life, had a daughter who loved him and a beautiful piece of land to call his own. Friedrich loved and was loved by many. I'd say those were full lives."

Evie wiped at her eyes and bit on her lip. "All of these bad things keep happening."

"And?"

"And I don't know if we can take much more."

He shrugged his shoulders. "Seems to me that you and Finch have each other. If you can weather these storms, you can handle anything else that comes your way."

"Mouse?"

"Yes."

"You're really smart."

"I have to be. When you're as small as me, you have to depend on other attributes. Lucky for me, I'm a genius." He winked at her and smiled.

***

Finch was the one who told Doris. He felt it was his place since he was there when it happened. Doris sobbed quietly when she heard the news. In all things in life, she was boisterous, loud, and her presence was always known, but in grief, she retreated into herself and suffered in silence.

"We can't leave him out there" she had whispered. It was the first time Evie had ever heard Doris speak in a quiet tone.

"I'll take care of it," Finch said. The phone lines were still down. Most of the town of Haines had been affected by the tornado in one way or another, and the power was still off inside of Evie's home.

Evie said in a quiet voice, "Take him to Mr. Boyd. He's the funeral director who took care of Daddy."

Finch gave her a quick nod.

Doris pressed her palm against his chest. "I want to see him before you take him anywhere."

"I don't think that's such a good idea," Finch said.

"Don't matter what you think. I want to see him," she said. "I'm going with you." She pushed the door open, glanced over her shoulder and said, "Are you coming?" Her face was paler than usual, and most of her make-up was smeared from when she had walked over in the rain. Her satin dress was wrinkled.

Finch reluctantly followed her out to the truck. Once they sat inside, he turned to face her. "It isn't pretty." He gulped.

She pinched his chin. "For a piss-ant, you sure are a sweetheart. Don't you worry about me: I'm a big girl. I can handle it."

He pressed his foot against the accelerator and drove toward the other side of the property.

When they reached the site, Finch eased the truck to a stop and turned off the engine. "You sure?" He figured he'd ask her one more time. Seeing how someone died, when it was tragic like it was with Friedrich, was something that burned in a person's brain, engraved itself, so years and years later it'd haunt them. He knew that image of Friedrich would pop up in his mind for years to come. He'd be working on a car or opening presents on Christmas day, and like a crow it'd gawk toward him, calling him, pecking him, and no matter how much he closed his eyes and tried to shut it out, the pull would be too much. It'd shine bright in his mind, making him relive the pain all over again. "Maybe you should wait until..." but before he could finish his sentence, Doris was out of the truck and ambling toward the fence bordering the property.

He ran to her and placed his arm around her shoulder. She kissed his hand and murmured, "Sweet boy."

He said nothing else, did nothing else and waited. Like a tick, tick, tick of a clock, he just sat there and waited for her reaction, holding his breath.

She moved a few steps and scanned the wreckage, placing her hand to her mouth. Her chest rose and fell flat, and she let out a loud sigh. "Poor people."

Poor people, he thought. But they lived. They lived.

She walked again and stopped at the fence, looking to Finch. "Help me over."

Finch quickly jumped the fence as she climbed onto the bottom rail. He extended his hand to hers as she heaved herself over. Her face turned red, and her breaths grew loud and heavy.

Once she was safely to the other side of the property, she stopped to take a few deep breaths and wiped her hands against her dress. "Ain't climbed a fence in years."

"Except that one time," Finch said and faintly smiled. They'd been in one town that wasn't keen on their presence and had to make a quick escape before people in town got to them. Finch remembered climbing a fence, rushing to his car, and Doris, who had weighed double at the time, struggling to get herself over the fence.

"They had torches," she said and laughed. "Wasn't funny at the time but it sure is now, ain't it?"

Finch agreed and smiled at the thought, thinking that people could be so ignorant, set in their ways, deciding who was normal, who wasn't, and then inflicting their rage against those who they didn't identify as their own.

He laughed, and Doris joined along. Finch swore he heard a sniffle within her guffaws. He scratched at his temple and looked down. "I don't know why it's so funny now."

"Sometimes all you can do is laugh at stupidity, Finch."

He grew serious and said, "We've really lived through it, haven't we?"

"I'd say so. Not too many people have been to as many places as we have and seen all that we have."

"I already miss him" Finch said.

Doris opened her arms wide and gestured to Finch. He fell against her chest and hugged her. "Me too, Honey Lamb. Me too." She let go of him and wrinkled her brow. "I need to see him," she whispered.

She offered her hand to Finch, and they headed toward Friedrich. She stopped when she saw him.

"Friedrich!" she cried out loud and rushed to him. She knelt beside him and bent down, pressing her body against his, to let out choked sobs.

***

He gave her the time she needed. Grief was a funny thing. Everyone handled it differently. Some retreated; others dealt with their pain publicly and asked for everyone to share in it. Doris showed her emotions in front of Finch but didn't ask for a shoulder to cry on or a hand to hold. Finch sat down against the fence letting her have her time to speak to Friedrich. She talked to him like he heard her even though he couldn't, but maybe he could. Maybe his spirit was fluttering nearby like a butterfly perching on wildflowers bringing its beauty to the world. Finch liked to think Friedrich could hear her. He didn't know what she was saying, but he imagined it was full of love and promise and all things that the two of them had shared.

He hadn't thought things through and worried that he wasn't going to be able to lift Friedrich's body and place him in the truck. He hoped he had some inner strength that wasn't there before because he couldn't ask Doris to help him. He just couldn't.

A man cleared his throat from behind him, and Finch turned to see who it was. Mr. Holt and a younger man were frowning at Finch, standing on Evie's property behind the fence.

Finch shot up and headed over to them.

"Evie told us what happened. We came to check on y'all," Mr. Holt said.

Finch nodded.

"We come to help you get him to the funeral home." He pointed politely, his finger never directly aimed in the direction of Friedrich, "This is my son, John. He's gonna help you lift the man."

John extended his hand to Finch, who shook it.

"She's saying her goodbyes," Finch whispered, and the two men knowingly nodded. They titled their heads and cast their lips down.

Mr. Holt looked up at Finch. "I'm real sorry. Evie told me what he done."

"He was a good man," Finch said. "People just judged him wrong because he was covered in tattoos," he said in a curt tone. Sure he was mad. He blamed the whole damn town.

"I'm sure they did. When I first heard he was living next door, I didn't know what to think," Mr. Holt said. "But I can be a fool sometimes."

"I guess we all can," Finch softened his tone. If the old man was going to recognize his ignorance, Finch could forgive him.

Doris made heavy, deliberate steps toward them and wiped at her eyes. Her chubby face was even puffier and rosy red. She offered a faint smile to Mr. Holt and John. Black mascara was smeared under her eyes and covered most of her plump cheeks.

"Hi," she said quietly.

"Hello," Mr. Holt said. "I'm real sorry for your loss, ma'am." He tipped his hat and nodded in a sign of respect.

Doris's grin grew slightly, and she said, "Ain't had a man tip his hat at me in a long time. That was a real nice gesture, mister. Thank you."

Holt offered his hand to her and said, "Need help over?"

She grabbed onto it and let herself over the fence. "Thank you." She breathed heavily and rubbed her hand under her nose. "That's mighty kind of you."

John stood on the fence rail and let himself over on the Myers' property. He made his way to Finch as Holt offered his arm to Doris and said, "This ain't something you need to see. How about I walk you back to Evie's house?"

"Okay," Doris said in a whisper. She placed her hand on his arm and glanced over her shoulder one more time, muttering something under her breath that only she could hear. Then she walked with Mr. Holt down the hill toward the house.

"On the count of three," Finch ordered as he and John struggled to get the ridge beam off of Friedrich. Their chests rose and fell flat. They bent over and pressed their palms against their knees as they panted like two dogs in heat.

After his body was freed, they carried Friedrich to the truck bed. Both out of breath and sweating profusely, they sat down on the grass for a moment and got themselves together.

"He must have had a big heart," John said.

"He did."

"There ain't too many men like him in this world."

"No there aren't."

Finch got up in the truck bed and knelt next to Friedrich's body. He closed Friedrich's eyes and pulled two quarters out of his pants pocket, placing them on Friedrich's eyes before he jumped down and sat in the driver's seat.

CHAPTER 19

"I've just about had it with funerals," Evie said with a glum face. She moved slowly, still feeling the effects of having broken ribs. She struggled to put on her sweater and gestured for Katie to help her.

Katie dried her tears and sucked in her round cheeks. "Me too, Eves. Me too." She looked down at her stomach, and her lips lifted. "He's kicking." She grabbed Evie's hand and pressed it against her. "Feel."

Even Evie couldn't deny the sheer amazement of it – that a human life was growing inside of Katie. "He's active," Evie said.

Katie wrapped her arms around Evie and squeezed. "I'll sure be glad when New Year's comes."

Evie side-glanced Katie.

"This has been one of the worst years of my life, and the sooner Dick Clark drops that ball the better."

"So much good has come our way, and so much bad has tainted it."

"Can't have it one way, you know?" She felt the curve of her belly. "Like this guy. I'm so happy to be having a baby. I just wish Momma would talk to me, and that I'd had enough sense to give this little man a better father."

"Your mom will come around. And Todd's an idiot."

"I should have known better. Guess you go scraping at the bottom of a barrel when you've got nothing but my daddy as an example." She let go of Evie.

Evie didn't say anything. The subject of Nate was a sore one, and she figured why dig into the wound when it was already opened and trying to heal. Evie just hoped that one day Nate would get what was coming to him. She prayed that people like him didn't coast through life without paying for their sins, but she knew that sometimes life played cruel tricks on people, and those who didn't deserve it suffered the most.

Finch rubbed his hands against his pants and fumbled with his tie. He untied it and retied it, trying to get it perfect. "Allow me," Evie said and tied it right for him. He gave her an appreciative smile and kissed her on the cheek.

"You're a keeper," he whispered.

"I guess I can say the same of you," she retorted with a smile. It felt good to smile. It'd been a while, and her eyes had just about had it with crying so much.

Emily tugged on Finch's hand and clasped her hand around his. "You look nice," she said.

"Thank you." It was the one nice pair of dress pants and shirt he'd owned. The tie was Gray's, which was the only tie Gray had owned, and given the differences in their sizes, it wasn't a surprise that it hung loosely around Finch's neck.

Doris' brown hair was teased and sprayed. Cornflower blue eyeshadow covered her thick eyelids and bright red lipstick adorned her plump lips. Two round spots of pink filled her cheeks. A satin pink bow was clipped to her hair, and her pink frock had been ironed. She smelled like lilac.

Mouse wore a gray plaid fedora, a black button-down shirt and a pair of gray slacks. His wing tip shoes shined in the sunlight.

Cooper's faded black pants and navy blue shirt were pressed. Evie didn't have the heart to tell him his shirt wasn't black—Cooper was color blind. She was thankful he was there, that he had come. He had arrived early that morning carrying a basket of fried chicken and a potted bird of paradise. "Momma made the chicken for y'all, and ain't this the prettiest plant you've ever seen?" he had said. He looked down at the floor and shook his head. "He was a real good man." Evie touched him on the arm, giving him a grateful look. He peered down at Emily and offered her a smile. "You're the spittin' image of Evie when she was a youngin'. You sure y'all ain't twins?"

Emily shook her head. "She's a lot older than me. We can't be twins."

Cooper grinned at her.

"Mr. Cooper is just gettin' your goat is all," Evie had said to her. "He was your daddy's best friend. You should've seen those two together."

Emily's eyes lit up. She was curious about Gray, and Evie was more than happy to tell her about him anytime she asked. When Evie tucked her in at night, she'd share a story about him. Emily would listen intently and beg her for more.

"Tell me a story about him," Emily had begged Cooper.

"Tell you what, you ride with me on the way and I'll tell you about the first time he and I met," he had said to her.

Cooper took a look at them all and said, "We're all smart looking, ain't we?"

"We sure are," Doris said, then twitched her lips and drummed her fingers against her dress. "Hope this preacher man don't muck up Friedrich's funeral. Sometimes preachers get all preachy and you end up losing the message 'cause they done gone off and turned it into a save your soul sermon."

"Reverend Simmerson isn't a hellfire and damnation type," Evie said. "No snakes or holy rolling with him."

"Good. Friedrich would've hated that," Doris said.

He pulled a few note cards out of his front pocket and made his way to the podium. He stood behind it and placed each note card out on it, straightening them into one nice neat row before he cleared his throat again and began to talk.

"Friedrich Adler was a good man," he said. Evie cringed from the cliché beginning. Starting a sermon with such a basic statement about a man who was so much more just seemed wrong to her somehow, and the longer she sat there and thought things through, the more sad her heart felt. No one was coming. The man deserved a grand funeral, full of life and people, an event that could put shame to Elvis' funeral.

Finch breathed heavy and played with his loose tie. His legs rocked back and forth, and his hands pressed against his pants, over and over. Evie had never seen him so nervous. She held onto him tighter and mouthed, "I love you" to him, hoping it'd quell the nerves. He gave her a grateful smile, then formed a slight frown.

She fought the tears, but feeling it all, seeing the pain it was causing him that no one had the decency to show their respect to Friedrich, was gut wrenching. She tried to save face, but it was too hard trying to fake it when everyone around her felt it.

A hacking cough rattled from the back of the funeral home, and Evie quickly turned around: it was Mr. Holt and his wife. They made eye contact with her and shuffled quickly to a nearby pew. Evie felt her heart lift.

One by one the townspeople of Haines began to trickle into the funeral home, and Finch quit fidgeting and gave a relieved smile to Evie. He was beaming. Reverend Simmerson stopped speaking and flickered a wide grin at the groups of people who were entering the funeral home. Everyone was there: the Myers family, Katie's mother, who came without Nate, Mr, Jacobs, who had called on Evie and Finch the moment he heard, then begged her to work for him. Evie couldn't refuse. "It's good money, more than I'd ever make raising these cows on my own," she had said to Finch. "And it's what I'm good at. I can still manage the farm, but I think I'd like to try this, too." Finch didn't argue. He was proud that his fiancé was finally getting paid what she was due. "Daddy would be proud," she had said.

When the pews filled, people stood, and a line formed outside of the funeral home. She turned around and motioned for Cooper to lean forward. "What do you think made them change their mind?" she whispered to him.

"Mr. and Mrs. Myers told some people about what Friedrich had done, and once word spread that he'd saved them, I guess they finally came to their senses." He shrugged and patted her on the shoulder. "It's good to know they ain't heartless, isn't it?"

Evie smiled as the room filled to capacity. Not a sound was heard except the smooth southern twang of Reverend Simmerson's voice. And so, Reverend Simmerson began his sermon again, this time omitting the cliché statement and telling everyone what a hero Friedrich Adler was.

After the funeral, a caravan of cars drove to Evie's house. She stood with Finch, Doris, Emily, Mouse and Katie on her front porch, watching lines of cars fill the driveway and the road in front of the house. Evie held onto Finch's hand as hoards of people walked on her land, carrying plates of food and bouquets of flowers.

"Look at all that food," Doris said. She wiped at her eyes and her lips curled upward into a smile. "We ain't gonna starve with all that food."

Preston was one of the first to arrive. He shook each of their hands. Evie watched him as he shook Katie's hand, holding it the way a politician would with his other hand cupped over hers.

"Did you try that salve I brought you?" he asked Katie, his hand still on hers.

"Yes. It helped." Evie noticed the color rising to Katie's cheeks and heard the squeaky pitch in her tone.

"I figured it would," he said. He scanned her up and down. "That boy doing okay?" He peered down at her stomach and then looked her directly in her eyes.

She averted her eyes and glanced at Evie, who failed to inconspicuously look in another direction.

Katie patted her stomach and smiled. "He is. He's kicking me right now."

Preston raised his brows.

"Want to feel?"

"Sure."

She grabbed his hand and placed it on her stomach. "He's feisty, isn't he?"

"He's strong," he said. "Like his momma."

Evie shifted so she wasn't facing them, wanting to give them their privacy even though they were out on the middle of her porch in front of God and everyone. As far as she knew, there was nothing between them, but from the looks on their faces and their roaming hands, it sure looked like something to her.

Townspeople continued to trickle in, filling the inside and outside of her home. "He's a real hero," more than one person said to them that day.

"I'm real sorry I didn't have the chance to know him," others said.

Mrs. Myers whispered into Logan's ear and gently pushed him toward Evie and Finch. She rested her hands on Logan's bony shoulders. He hesitated and looked up and over his shoulder, giving his mother an uncertain look. She made a gesture to him, the kind that said for him to start talking. He twisted his lips to the side. He wouldn't make eye contact and brought his fingers up to his mouth and bit on the loose pieces of skin.

"I'm sorry for all that I've done," he said.

His mother pressed her hands firmly on his shoulders.

"And," he sucked in some air, "I didn't know your bull was going to die. We just thought it'd be fun to take him on Mr. Holt's property." Tears trickled down from his beady eyes. "I really didn't know. Promise."

Evie's heart skipped a beat. She had to take a deep breath to calm herself. She'd always suspected that he was the reason Miles had died. Now she had the proof. The question was, what was she going to do about it?

Mrs. Myers whispered in his ears. "And I'm sorry I wrote all that stuff and hit my golf balls on your property."

Evie couldn't say it was okay because it wasn't, but she couldn't be a hypocrite and not forgive him, either. She turned to Finch to read his reaction, and he closed his lips together and breathed through his nose.

Finally, he opened his mouth and said, "We're going to move on." He wrapped his arm around Evie and added, "We're starting fresh." He offered his hand to Logan, who slowly extended his and shook Finch's, giving him a weak handshake in comparison to Finch's. He quickly jetted off, far enough away from Evie and Finch.

"I'm very sorry," Mrs. Myers said. "So sorry."

Finch held up his palm. "Let's just move on."

"We appreciate all you've done for us. Friedrich saved our lives. I'm sorry I didn't get the chance to know him," she said reflectively.

"He was the best," Finch said. "You would've liked him." He decided not to point out that she never gave Friedrich the chance. It was time to move on. He hoped she'd learn from it – that maybe she'd open her heart to someone she considered different instead of shutting the door on them. It was his hope, at least, that it would.

She nodded once and scooted away from them.

"How do you respond to that?" Evie asked Finch. "Because I didn't want to say it was okay because it's not, but I can't not forgive him."

He rolled his shoulders. "You don't respond." He sighed. "He said he's sorry. We just have to forgive and forget."

She blinked her blue eyes and half-smiled. "I guess we do, don't we?"

Mike approached them, his hat held in his hands and he peered down at the floor. "I'm real sorry for your loss."

"Thanks for coming," Finch said. He wanted to add that he'd missed him.

"I come to pay my respects and to see if you'd consider working for me again."

Finch's face lit up, and Evie garnered a wide grin.

"Consider it?" Finch repeated. "There's no need, 'cause I'll be there the day you want me to start."

"Tomorrow sound good?" Mike beamed. "'Cause I sure could use the help. I've missed having you around." He nudged Finch and grinned.

"How about a few days from now? I've got some pressing

business that can't wait." He squeezed Evie's hand.

"Sounds good. I look forward to it," Mike said and started in the opposite direction then spun around. "I was wrong, Finch. Real wrong."

Finch held up his hand. "Let bygones be bygones."

"Still... all the same, it wasn't right what the town had done, and I should've stuck up for you instead of letting them bully me. I'm sorry," he said.

"It's forgotten," Finch said. "I'll be back at work in a few days. Can you do me a favor?"

"Anything," Mike said.

"Find a new station on that radio of yours. I'd like to hear some music from this decade while I work," Finch said and smiled.

"It only plays the one station," Mike shot back and nudged him again before walking away.

"Pressing business?" Evie said.

"There's this woman I'm madly in love with who I'm dying to make my wife."

"I'd say that sounds like really important business," she said. "In fact, I'd say that this business needs to be taken care of immediately."

CHAPTER 20

Evie checked her reflection one more time and turned to Katie, Doris and Emily. "How do I look?"

Katie wiped at her eyes. "Like a million bucks, Eves."

"Who you kiddin', Honey Lamb? You'd look good with dog poo poo all over you," Doris added. "You look good, Honey Lamb. Real good."

"You look really pretty," Emily said. She sat on the rocking chair in Evie's bedroom and kicked her legs back and forth.

"I'd say you're the prettiest flower girl a bride can have," Evie said to her. They weren't close or inseparable, but time and circumstances were bringing them closer, and Evie knew it'd only be a matter of time until things were seamless between them.

Emily's eyes sparkled, and she touched the lace on her floral print dress.

Evie's long blonde hair was tied up into a nice chic bun. Blonde ringlets surrounded her face. Katie had worked hours on it. Blue eye shadow tinted her eyelids, and pink blush and lipstick adorned her cheeks and lips.

Katie sprayed Aqua Net hair spray onto Evie's hair one more time, and Evie closed her eyes and coughed. "You've about used that entire can," she said.

"We need to make sure it stays put." Katie patted the top of Evie's head, which refused to move with the less than delicate touch of her hand. "Good enough." She nodded in confidence. She grabbed hold of Evie's face once more and scanned her over. "Just a little more blush." She brought out a brush and applied another coat of the rose colored blush to Evie's cheeks.

Doris pinned baby's breath into Evie's hair and said, "This makes it perfect."

Evie slowly got up and turned around, looking down at her white dress. "You think this is okay for a wedding dress?"

Katie and Doris vigorously nodded their heads. "Honey Lamb, he's going to pop his eyes out of his sockets when he sees you." Doris had stayed busy planning the wedding immediately after the funeral when Finch and Evie announced they were going to get married. She and Katie worked through the night cooking, cleaning, and making sure everything was perfect for their special day. "It gets my mind off of Friedrich," she had said. "Glad something good is coming from all of this."

Doris, Katie, Emily and Evie had gone shopping the day before to try and find Evie and Emily dresses. Evie refused to wear her grandmother's wedding dress—it had hung in the closet collecting dust. Gray had saved it for her, saying it was a family heirloom, but all Evie saw was a sheet of lace. "It's morbid and looks like death with all that lace."

Her cream colored satin gown hit her at her knees. The v-neck neck line gave a glimpse of her cleavage, and her sleeves fluttered as she moved about the room. The dress was simple and chic – exactly what she had wanted in a wedding dress.

Evie placed her arm against her chest. "These dern ribs are killing me."

"Y'all's honeymoon sure will be interesting with those broken ribs of yours," Doris said. "The term 'be gentle' will have a double meaning."

Evie shot her a look, side-glancing at Emily. "Doris," she admonished.

Doris laughed. "Wonder how ole Finchy is doing?" she said. "Bet he's a basket of nerves."

Evie chewed on a nail and then stopped when she saw Katie giving her the evil eye.

"He's probably not as nervous as me," Evie said and took a deep breath.

Doris cupped her chin and smiled. "Honey Lamb, he'd move Heaven and Earth for you. I ain't ever seen him so helpless before. You done stole his heart. I'd say getting married to you is going to send him over the edge."

Evie's cheeks turned a rosier shade, and her lips raised upward. She inhaled and said quietly, "I've never been happier in my life."

***

Finch fiddled with his neck tie—attempting to tie it right—and cursed under his breath. He turned to Rolf, who had rushed to South Carolina the moment Finch called him to tell him he and Evie were tying the knot. "Let me," Rolf said and tied the sea blue tie —the color was Evie's request—around Finch's neck.

"Thanks." Finch cleared his throat and paced. He looked upward at the ceiling, then back at Rolf, Mouse and Stoney. Stoney had insisted on tagging along with Rolf, saying he wouldn't miss Finch's wedding to that sweet girl even if he was coughing up blood and had a fever of one hundred and ten. Finch didn't bother to tell him that having such a temperature was impossible. He appreciated that two of his oldest friends had dropped everything so that they could share in his joy.

He looked off in the distance for a minute and felt the pressure of Rolf's hand on his shoulders.

"He's here in spirit," Rolf said, reading Finch's mind.

"I just wish he could be here today," Finch said.

"Me too," he said quietly. "Do you have the rings?"

Finch felt around his pants pocket. "Yes."

"Good. Last wedding I went to, the groom forgot the rings."

"I double-checked behind him," Mouse said.

"You're pacing around like a drunk without his hooch," Stoney said to Finch.

Finch stopped. "Don't know why I'm so nervous."

"You're getting married. You don't want to muck this up," Mouse said. "And you won't, so quit squirreling around 'cause it's making us seasick."

Rolf and Stoney agreed. "I'm going to smoke a cigarette. I can't handle it no more." Stoney stepped outside and lit up on the front porch.

Cooper tapped on the door and then let himself inside. He was dressed in a pair of pressed khaki pants and a wide-collared yellow shirt.

"You cleaned up," Finch said. He smelled his aftershave and noticed Cooper had combed his hair and shined his boots.

"Can't go walking my girl down the aisle dressed like a hobo," he said. "Had to go to Sears in Chester to get this outfit."

"Well, you cleaned up good, Coop. I didn't know you had it in you," Finch said.

"Gotta do her daddy proud since he can't be here." He started to get choked up and then let out a soft sigh. "Ain't going to stand here and cry on y'alls wedding day. Where is she?"

"Upstairs getting dressed," Finch answered.

"Guess I better be getting up there to do my job." Cooper started up the steps.

"Well, shall we?" Finch said to Rolf, Stoney and Mouse.

They walked outside to take their posts. Ernie and his band had offered to play at the wedding. "No charge," they said, and Finch and Evie didn't argue. Free was free, and if they could get entertainment and someone to play "The Wedding March" half-way decently, then they'd take them up on their offer.

A crowd of onlookers stood near the big elm tree, the one Evie loved so much. It was a brisk day, but the sun was shining, and there wasn't a cloud in the sky. Ernie and his band played a simple melody, some unknown forgotten tune from years before.

Finch stood with his hands in his pockets, fidgeting like he'd drunk gallons of caffeine, but he couldn't calm himself. His heart was fluttering, and the more he waited for Evie to walk down those porch steps toward him, the faster his heart beat. He'd never wanted something so bad in his entire life.

For anyone attending the wedding, they could say with all certainty that it was the most unique wedding party they'd ever seen: old, retired carnies as groomsmen and a carny and a pregnant woman as bridesmaids.

***

Cooper knocked on Evie's door. "It's me, Cooper."

She laughed. "Coop, I know your voice, and what other man would be knocking on this door on my wedding day? Come on in," she said, and the moment he opened the door and saw Evie all dolled up and in her wedding gown, he sobbed.

"Quit crying, Coop, or you'll ruin my make-up," Evie said, sniffling. She dabbed at her eyes with a tissue.

He wiped at his eyes with the sleeve of his shirt. "Can't help it. You look beautiful, and your daddy would be proud that you're marrying such a good man. You picked a good one."

Evie placed her hand against her chest and smiled. "Now that's the nicest thing you've ever said to me, Coop. You gotta quit crying so we can get on with this ceremony. Otherwise, I'm never going to get married to Finch."

"Fair enough. I'm honored you want me to walk you down the aisle," he said.

She took a deep breath and wiped at her eyes again. "You gotta stop saying all this sweet stuff or I'm going to be a blubbering mess. Besides, who else is good enough to walk me down?"

"No one." He thrust his chest out proudly. "Ain't no one else I can think of."

"Well," she gestured for them all to come toward her, "I'm not much for hugging, but I'm feeling the love bug today." They encircled Evie and stretched their arms out wide to hug her. Emily wrapped her small arms around Evie's waist and looked up at her.

"I'm glad my sister and closest friends are here to see me get married," she said.

"This is getting real sappy. We keep at it, we'll be joining hands and singing folk songs," Doris said. "Time to get." She motioned for Katie and Emily to follow her downstairs.

Cooper extended his arm out to Evie. "You ready?"

"I've never been so ready in my life, Coop."

***

Finch and Evie stood facing each other, holding hands. A small crowd of close friends surrounded them, and Mouse, Stoney, Rolf, Doris, Katie, and Emily were by their sides as they exchanged vows they'd personally written. "I'm not going to be a puppet and repeat what the preacher says I'm supposed to say, and I refuse to say the word 'obey'," Evie had said.

Finch had told her, "Well then, let's write our own vows, then you can say whatever is inside of that random head of yours."

"Finch, do you take Evie to be your wife?" Reverend Simmerson asked.

"Yes," he answered and laced his fingers through Evie's. "From the moment I met you, I knew you were different, and then when I grew to know you, I couldn't help but fall in love. Evie," he tugged on her hands and looked deep into her blue eyes. "You're like all things beautiful, and I love you. I promise to love you with all of my being each and every day until I die. I'll treat you with respect and will be there for you when you need me."

"And do you, Evie, take Finch to be your husband?" Reverend Simmerson asked.

She laced her fingers with his and said, "Finch, we had a rocky start, didn't we?" They both laughed. "But I couldn't help but want to know you, and knowing you better meant falling in love with you. You're the reason I can't wait to get up in the morning. I cherish every moment we spend together. You're my best friend, and I love you. I promise to love you unconditionally and will be by your side always." They continued to stare into each other's eyes and held onto each other's hands, waiting for Reverend Simmerson to pronounce them as husband and wife.

When they finished their vows, sniffling was heard, and Evie and Finch swore that there wasn't a dry eye amongst the guests.

"Finch and Evie, I now pronounce you husband and wife," Reverend Simmerson said. A round of applause erupted, along with a few cheers, mostly from Cooper and Doris.

Finch and Evie formed lovestruck goofy grins —from ear to ear

—and squeezed their hands together.

"Y'all can kiss now," Reverend Simmerson added.

"Kiss me hard, Finch," Evie said, blinking her long eyelashes and giving him an impish grin.

"Come here, you," Finch said with a smile. "You're my forever," he whispered before he pressed his lips on hers.

EPILOGUE

MAY, 1979

Evie rushed inside and scanned the area, searching for Katie. She saw the back of her head and moved through the crammed courtroom to get to her. There wasn't an empty seat in the entire room, with the exception of the small space Katie saved for Evie.

"Sorry I'm late. There was a problem with one of Mr. Jacobs' cows," she whispered to her breathlessly. Her chest heaved outward and inward. "I sped to get here."

Katie picked up her pocket book, placed it in her lap and pointed to the space for Evie to take a seat. "It's okay. Nothing's happened yet," she whispered back.

Evie glanced around Katie and smiled. "Hi, Preston."

He smiled at her. "Hey, Evie."

"Have you talked to him yet?" Evie whispered with a hiss to Katie, nodding toward the front of the court room.

She twisted her lips to the side. "No, not yet. I'm having a hard enough time looking at him," she said.

"All rise," the bailiff said, and Katie and Evie both stood up. "The Honorable Jenson Vaughn proceeding."

"In the case of the state of South Carolina versus Nathaniel James McDaniels, the state would like to call their first witness, Preston Dobbins, to the stand," said the prosecuting attorney.

"That's me," Preston said in a soft voice to Katie. He patted her on the leg and then placed his hands on the wheels to his wheel chair and moved forward.

He made his way in front of the witness stand and placed his hand on the Holy Bible. "Do you swear to the tell truth, the whole truth, so help you God?" the bailiff asked.

"I do," Preston said.

"Can you state your name for the court?"

"Preston August Dobbins."

"And what is your occupation?"

"I was a Federal Drug Enforcement Administration Agent."

THE END

THE HEARTS OF HAINES SERIES CONTINUES

Check out the sequel, *This is Where We Begin*.

In this continuation in the Hearts of Haines Series, Katie McDaniels is unemployed, pregnant, and relying on Evie and Finch for a place to live. She is trying to survive. Nothing seems to be going right for her until Preston Dobbins steps into her life and an unexpected gift comes her way, finally giving her a chance at happiness.

Preston Dobbins is fighting his strong feelings for Katie McDaniels. He guards a well-kept secret, one that consumes him with guilt.

As an old foe threatens Katie's happiness, Preston risks everything to save her from tragedy.

OTHER BOOKS BY THIS AUTHOR:

The Summer I Learned to Dive.

Since the time she was a little girl, eighteen-year-old Finley "Finn" Hemmings has always lived her life according to a plan, focused and driven with no time for the average young adult's carefree experiences. On the night of her high school graduation, things take a dramatic turn when she discovers that her mother has been keeping a secret from her—a secret that causes Finn to do something she had never done before—veer off her plan. In the middle of the night, Finn packs her bags and travels by bus to Graceville, SC seeking the truth. In Graceville, Finn has experiences that change her life forever; a summer of love, forgiveness and revelations. She learns to take chances, to take the plunge and to dive right in to what life has to offer.

The Year I Almost Drowned.

In this continuation of "The Summer I Learned to Dive," nineteen-year old Finley "Finn" Hemmings is living in Graceville, South Carolina with her grandparents. She's getting to know the family that she was separated from for the last sixteen years. Finn and Jesse's relationship seems to be going strong until they're forced to deal with obstacles that throw them off-track. As Finn prepares to leave for college, she has to say goodbye to the town, her friends and family, and the way of life that she has grown to love.

At college, Finn tries to acclimate to a new setting, but quickly falls into an old pattern. Just as things start to become normal and Finn begins to fit in, something unexpected happens that takes her back to Graceville where she is forced to deal with one challenge after another. Her world nearly collapses, and she finds herself struggling to keep from drowning. Through it all, Finn discovers the power of love and friendship. She learns what it means to follow her heart and to stay true to what she wants, even if what she wants isn't what she originally planned.

<u>The Days Lost</u>.

On the heels of her high school graduation, Ellie Morales is spending her summer vacation in the mountains of Western North Carolina with her dad and brother, Jonah. Having lost their mother only months earlier, all of them are trying to cope with the loss in their own way. Part routine, part escape, running is Ellie's way of dealing with her grief. Shortly after sunrise each morning, Ellie and her dog, Bosco, set out for a lengthy run on the path that passes by her house and leads deep into the woods of the Blue Ridge Mountains. One fateful morning, Ellie is lead off of the trail and discovers a secret that will change her life, as well as the lives of the family she meets, forever. One member of this mysterious family is Sam Gantry, who seems unlike any guy she's ever known. This meeting sparks a series of events, causing Ellie to question everything she's ever known and believed. The more she learns about Sam and his family, the more she wants to help him find the missing puzzle pieces.

ABOUT THE AUTHOR

Shannon McCrimmon was born and raised in Central Florida. She earned a Master's Degree in Counseling from Rollins College. In 2008, she moved to the upstate of South Carolina. It was the move to the upstate that inspired her to write novels. Shannon lives in Greenville, South Carolina with her husband and toy poodle.

Did you enjoy *Like All Things Beautiful?* Please consider supporting the author by writing a review on Amazon.com or Goodreads.com.

Interested in learning more about my upcoming projects? Sign up to receive my newsletter at http://bit.ly/Ma0iSJ Become a fan at www.facebook.com/shannonmccrimmonauthor or follow me on twitter@smccrimmon1

ACKNOWLEDGEMENTS

Chris, thank you for your brainstorming sessions, for supporting me, and for listening to me read the entire story out loud, then offering me your two cents to make it a stronger, better story. You are my idea guru! I love you with all of my heart, and I'm one lucky woman to have a husband like you. Laurin, you are a true friend and a great editor. I appreciate all of your support and enthusiasm for each and every book that I write. Everyone should have a friend like you. To my beta readers: Betty Jones, Wendy Wilken, and Joy McNeill, thank you so much for your feedback. You helped make this story even better. To the bloggers, Indie authors, and readers who have acted as champion supporters, I appreciate you. Thank you! To my family and friends who have supported me with my writing endeavors throughout the years, thank you. A special note of gratitude goes to my beautiful cousins: Victoria and Ashleigh. I love y'all. To everyone in my Awesome group on Facebook, you know who you are, and I am thankful for your support. To the Lee's, thank you for information about all things cattle. I would have messed up that calf birthing scene if it wasn't for Gordon's insight. And, of course, thank you for inspiring me with your beautiful property. To Stephanie Roach, thank you for assisting me with writing the blurb. Your honesty and feedback were immensely helpful. To all of the readers who've written me kind notes or have encouraged others to read my books, thank you.

Made in the USA
Charleston, SC
08 May 2015